Arabella Burton Buckley

Through Magic Glasses And Other Lectures

A Sequel to The Fairyland of Science

Arabella Burton Buckley

Through Magic Glasses And Other Lectures
A Sequel to The Fairyland of Science

ISBN/EAN: 9783744744065

Printed in Europe, USA, Canada, Australia, Japan

Cover: Foto ©Andreas Hilbeck / pixelio.de

More available books at **www.hansebooks.com**

THROUGH
MAGIC GLASSES

AND OTHER LECTURES

A SEQUEL TO THE FAIRYLAND OF SCIENCE

BY

ARABELLA B. BUCKLEY

(MRS. FISHER)

AUTHOR OF LIFE AND HER CHILDREN, WINNERS IN LIFE'S RACE,
A SHORT HISTORY OF NATURAL SCIENCE, ETC.

WITH NUMEROUS ILLUSTRATIONS

NEW YORK
D. APPLETON AND COMPANY
1890

PREFACE.

THE present volume is chiefly intended for those of my young friends who have read, and been interested in, the *Fairyland of Science*. It travels over a wide field, pointing out a few of the marvellous facts which can be studied and enjoyed by the help of optical instruments. It will be seen at a glance that any one of the subjects dealt with might be made the study of a lifetime, and that the little information given in each lecture is only enough to make the reader long for more.

In these days, when moderate-priced instruments and good books and lectures are so easily accessible, I hope some eager minds may be thus led to take up one of the branches of science opened out to us by magic glasses ; while those who go no further will at least understand something of the hitherto unseen world which is now being studied by their help.

The two last lectures wander away from this path, and yet form a natural conclusion to the Magician's lectures to his young Devonshire lads. They have been published before, one in the *Youth's Companion* of Boston, U.S., and the other in *Atalanta*, in which the essay on Fungi also appeared in a shorter form. All three lectures have, however, been revised and fully illustrated, and I trust that the volume, as a whole, may prove a pleasant Christmas companion.

For the magnificent photograph of Orion's nebula, forming the Frontispiece, I am indebted to the courtesy of Mr. Isaac Roberts, F.R.A.S., who most kindly lent me the plate for reproduction ; and I have had the great good fortune to obtain permission from MM. Henri of the Paris Observatory to copy the illustration of the Lunar Apennines from a most beautiful and perfect photograph of part of the moon, taken by them only last March. My cordial thanks are also due to Mr. A. Cottam, F.R.A.S., for preparing the plate of coloured double stars, and to my friend Mr. Knobel, Hon. Sec. of the R.A.S., for much valuable assistance ; to Mr. James Geikie for the loan of some illustrations from his *Geology ;* and to

Messrs. Longman for permission to copy Herschel's fine drawing of Copernicus.

With the exception of these illustrations and a few others, three of which were kindly given me by Messrs. Macmillan, all the woodcuts have been drawn and executed under the superintendence of Mr. Carreras, jun., who has made my task easier by the skill and patience he has exercised under the difficulties incidental to receiving instructions from a distance.

ARABELLA B. BUCKLEY.

UPCOTT AVENEL, *Oct.* 1890.

TABLE OF CONTENTS

CHAPTER VII

CHAPTER VIII

CHAPTER IX

CHAPTER X

LIST OF ILLUSTRATIONS

PLATES

WOODCUTS IN THE TEXT

2

THROUGH MAGIC GLASSES

CHAPTER I

THE MAGICIAN'S CHAMBER BY MOONLIGHT

THE full moon was shining in all its splendour one lovely August night, as the magician sat in his turret chamber bathed in her pure white beams, which streamed upon him through the open shutter in the wooden dome above. It is true a faint gleam of warmer light shone from below through the open door, for this room was but an offshoot at the top of the building, and on looking down the turret stairs a lecture-room might be seen below where a bright light was burning. Very little, however, of this warm glow reached the magician, and the implements of his art around him looked like weird gaunt skeletons as they cast their long shadows across the floor in the moonlight.

The small observatory, for such it was, was a circular building with four windows in the walls, and roofed with a wooden dome, so made that it could be shifted round and round by pulling certain cords. One section of this dome was a shutter, which now stood open, and the strip, thus laid bare to the night, was so turned as to face that part of the sky along which the moon was moving. In the centre of the room, with its long tube directed towards the opening, stood the largest magic glass, the TELESCOPE, and in the dead stillness of the night, could be heard distinctly the tick-tick of the clockwork, which kept the instrument pointing to the face of the moon, while the room, and all in it, was being carried slowly and steadily onwards by the earth's rotation on its axis. It was only a moderate-sized instrument, about six feet long, mounted on a solid iron pillar firmly fixed to the floor and fitted with the clockwork, the sound of which we have mentioned ; yet it looked like a giant as the pale moonlight threw its huge shadow on the wall behind and the roof above.

Far away from this instrument in one of the windows, all of which were now closed with shutters, another instrument was dimly visible. This was a round iron table with clawed feet, and upon it, fastened by screws, were three tubes, so arranged that they all pointed towards the centre of the table, where six glass prisms were arranged in a semicircle, each one fixed on a small brass tripod. A strange uncanny-looking instrument this, especially as the prisms caught the edge of the glow streaming up the turret stair, and shot forth faint beams of coloured light on the table below them. Yet the magician's pupils thought it still more uncanny and mysterious when their master used it to read the alphabet of light, and to discover by vivid lines even the faintest trace of a metal otherwise invisible to mortal eye.

For this instrument was the SPECTROSCOPE, by which he could break up rays of light and make them tell him from what substances they came. Lying around it were other curious prisms mounted in metal rims and fitted with tubes and many strange devices, not to be understood by the uninitiated, but magical in their effect when fixed on to the telescope and used to break up the light of distant stars and nebulæ.

Compared with these mysterious glasses the PHOTO-GRAPHIC CAMERA, standing in the background, with its tall black covering cloth, like a hooded monk, looked comparatively natural and familiar, yet it, too, had puzzling plates and apparatus on the table near it, which could be fitted on to the telescope, so that by their means pictures might be taken even in the dark night, and stars, invisible with the strongest lens, might be forced to write their own story, and leave their image on the plate for after study.

All these instruments told of the magician's power in unveiling the secrets of distant space and exploring realms unknown, but in another window, now almost hidden in the shadow, stood a fourth and highly-prized helpmate, which belonged in one sense more to our earth, since everything examined by it had to be brought near, and lie close under its magnifying-glass. Yet the MICROSCOPE too could carry its master into an unseen world, hidden to mortal eye by minuteness instead of by distance. If in the stillness of night the telescope was his most cherished servant and familiar friend, the microscope by day opened out to him the fairyland of nature.

As he sat on his high pedestal stool on this summer night with the moonlight full upon him, his whole attention was centred on the telescope, and his mind was far away from that turret-room, wandering into the distant space brought so near to him ; for he was waiting to watch an event which brought some new interest every time it took place —a total eclipse of the moon. To-night he looked forward to it eagerly, for it happened that, just as the moon would pass into the shadow of our earth, it would also cross directly in front of a star, causing what is known as an "occultation" of the star, which would disappear suddenly behind the rim of the dark moon, and after a short time flash out on the other side as the satellite went on its way.

How he wished as he sat there that he could have shown this sight to all the eager lads whom he was teaching to handle and love his magic glasses. For this magician was not only a student himself, he was a rich man and the Founder and Principal of a large public school for boys of the artisan class. He had erected a well-planned and handsome building in the midst of the open country, and received there, on terms within the means of their parents, working-lads from all parts of England, who, besides the usual book-learning, received a good technical education in all its branches. And, while he left to other masters the regular school lessons, he kept for himself the intense pleasure of opening the minds of these lads to the wonders of God's universe around them.

You had only to pass down the turret stairs, into the large science class-room below, to see at once that a loving hand and heart had furnished it. Not only was there every implement necessary for scientific work, but numerous rough diagrams covering the walls showed that labour as well as money had been spent in decorating them. It was a large oblong room, with four windows to the north, and four to the south, in each of which stood a microscope with all the tubes, needles, forceps, knives, etc., necessary for dissecting and preparing objects; and between the windows were open shelves, on which were ranged chemicals of various kinds, besides many strange-looking objects in bottles, which would have amused a trained naturalist, for the lads collected and preserved whatever took their fancy.

On some of the tables were photographic plates laid ready for printing off; on others might be seen drawings of the spectrum, made from the small spectroscope fixed at one end of the room; on others lay small direct spectroscopes which the lads could use for themselves. But nowhere was a telescope to be seen. This was not because there were none, for each table had its small hand-telescope, cheap but good. The truth is that each of these instruments had been spirited away into the dormitories that night, and many heads were lying awake on their pillows, listening for the strike of the clock to spring out and see the eclipse begin.

A mere glance round the room showed that the moon had been much studied lately.   On the blackboard was drawn a rough diagram, showing how a boy can illustrate for himself the moon's journey round the earth, by taking a ball and holding it a little above his head at arm's length, while he turns slowly round on his heel in a darkened room before

Fig. 1.

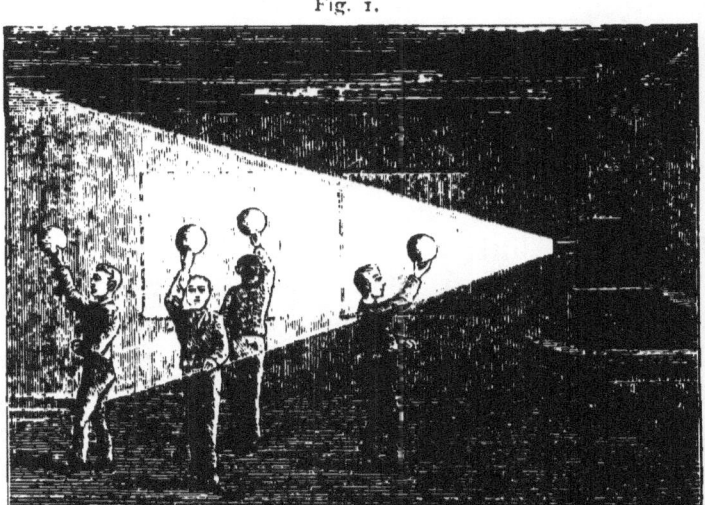

A boy illustrating the phases of the moon.

a lighted lamp, or better still before the lens of a magic lantern (Fig. 1).   The lamp or lens then represents the sun, the ball is the moon, the boy's head is the earth.   Beginning with the ball between him and the source of light, but either a little above, or a little below the direct line between his eye and it, he will see only the dark side of the ball, and the moon will be on the point of being " new." Then as he turns slowly, a thin crescent of light will creep over the side nearest the sun, and by degrees encroach more and more, so that when he has turned through one quarter of the round half the disc will be light. When he has turned another quarter, and has his back to the sun, a full moon will face him. Then as he turns on through the third quarter a crescent of darkness creeps slowly over the side away from the sun, and gradually the bright disc is eaten away by shadow till at the end of the third quarter half the disc again only is light ; then, when he has turned through another quarter and completed the circle, he faces the light again and has a dark moon before him. But he must take care to keep the moon a little above or a little below his eye at new and full moon. If he brings it exactly on a line with himself and the light at new moon, he will shut off the light from himself and see the dark body of the ball against the light, causing an *eclipse* of the sun ; while if he does the same at full moon his head will cast a shadow on the ball causing an *eclipse* of the moon.

There were other diagrams showing how and why such eclipses do really happen at different times in the moon's path round the earth ; but perhaps the most interesting of all was one he had made to explain what so few people understand, namely, that though the moon describes a complete circle round our earth every month, yet she does not describe a circle in space, but a wavy line inwards and out-

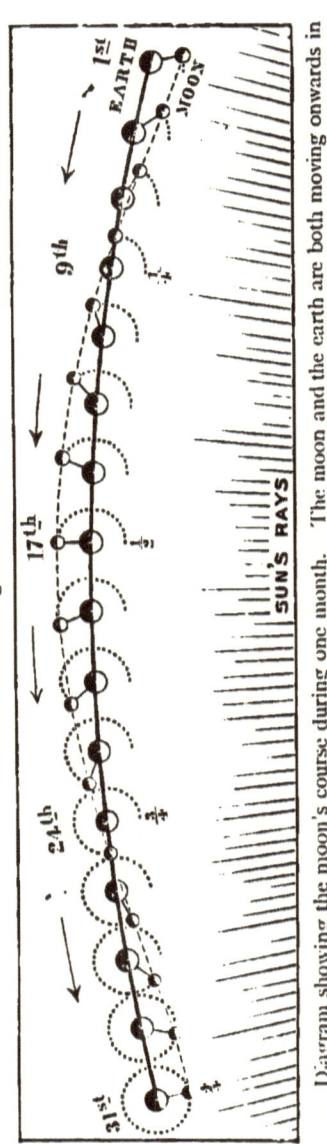

Fig. 2.

Diagram showing the moon's course during one month. The moon and the earth are both moving onwards in the direction of the arrows. The earth moves along the dark line, the moon along the interrupted line ‑‑‑‑. The dotted curved line .... shows the circle gradually described by the moon round the earth as they move onwards.

wards across the earth's path round the sun. This is because the earth is moving on all the while, carrying the moon with it, and it is only by seeing it drawn before our eyes that we can realise how it happens.

Thus suppose, in order to make the dates as simple as possible, that there is a new moon on the 1st of some month. Then by the 9th (or roughly speaking in $7\frac{3}{4}$ days) the moon will have described a quarter of a circle round the earth as shown by the dotted line (Fig. 2), which marks her position night after night with regard to us. Yet because she is carried onwards all the while by the earth, she will really have passed along the interrupted line - - - between us and the sun. During the next week her quarter of a circle will carry her round behind the earth, so that we see her on the 17th as a full moon, yet her actual movement has been onwards along the interrupted line on the farther side of the earth. During the third week she creeps round another quarter of a circle so as to be in advance of the earth on its yearly journey round the sun, and reaches the end of her third quarter on the 24th. In her last quarter she gradually passes again between the earth and the sun ; and though, as regards the earth, she appears to be going back round to the same place where she was at the beginning of the month, and on the 31st is again a dark new moon, yet she has travelled onwards exactly as much as we have, and therefore has really not described a circle in the *heavens* but a wavy line.

Near to this last diagram hung another, well loved by the lads, for it was a large map of the *face* of the moon, that is of the side which is *always* turned towards us, because the moon turns once on her axis during the month that she is travelling round the earth. On this map were marked all the different craters, mountains, plains and shining streaks which appear on the moon's face ; while round the chart were pictures of some of these at sunrise and sunset on the moon, or during the long day of nearly a fortnight which each part of the face enjoys in its turn.

By studying this map, and the pictures, they were able, even in their small telescopes, to recognise Tycho and Copernicus, and the mountains of the moon, after they had once grown accustomed to the

Fig. 3.

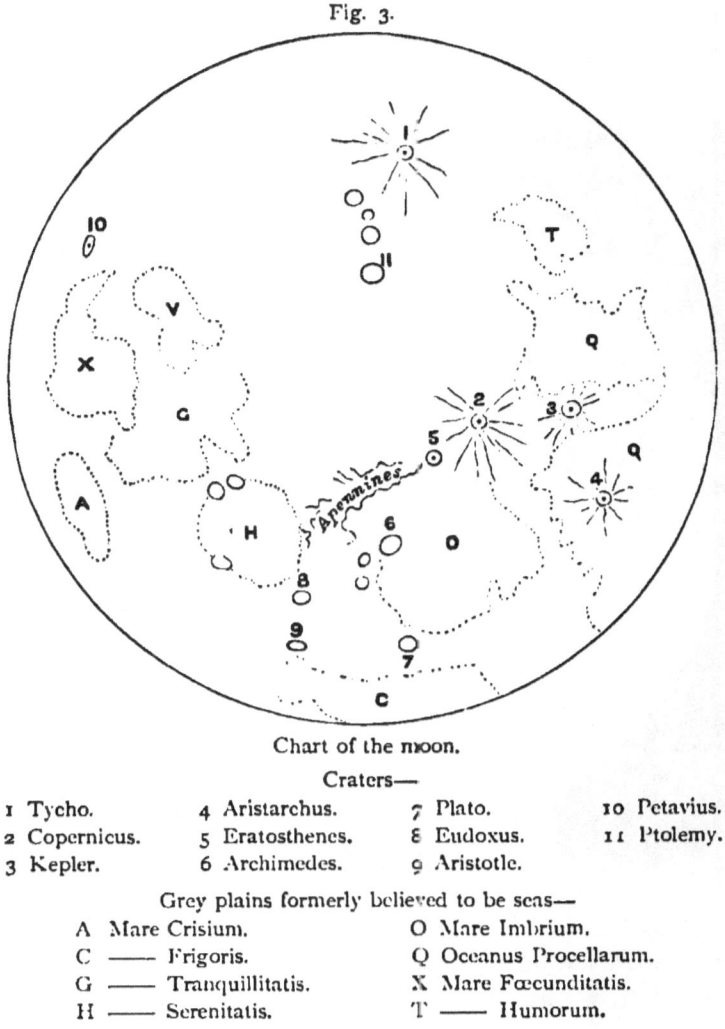

Chart of the moon.

Craters—

1 Tycho.	4 Aristarchus.	7 Plato.	10 Petavius.
2 Copernicus.	5 Eratosthenes.	8 Eudoxus.	11 Ptolemy.
3 Kepler.	6 Archimedes.	9 Aristotle.	

Grey plains formerly believed to be seas—

A Mare Crisium.	O Mare Imbrium.
C —— Frigoris.	Q Oceanus Procellarum.
G —— Tranquillitatis.	X Mare Fœcunditatis.
H —— Serenitatis.	T —— Humorum.

strange changes in their appearance which take

place as daylight or darkness creeps over them. They could not however pick out more than some of the chief points. Only the magician himself knew every crater and ridge under all its varying lights,

Fig. 3a.

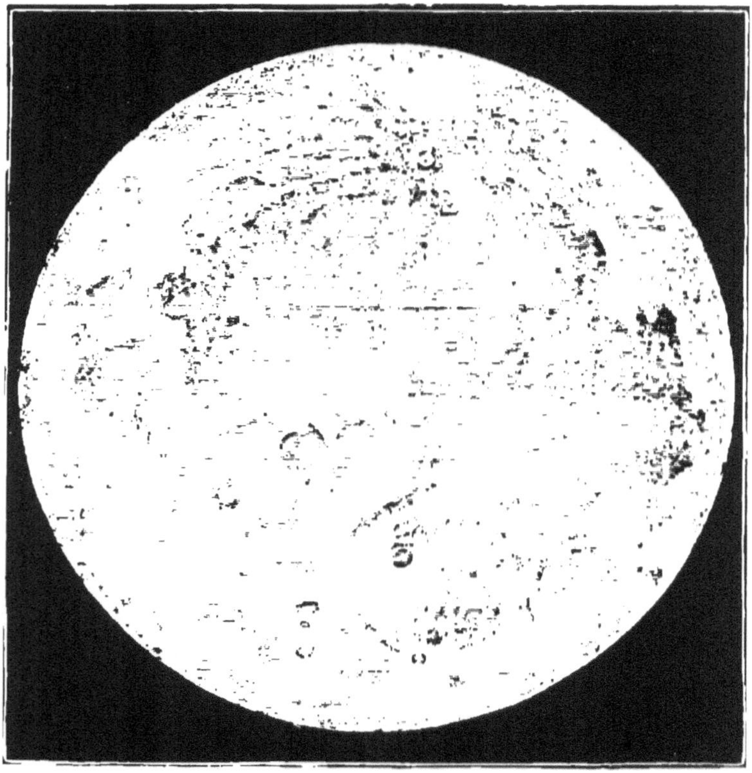

The full moon. (From Ball's *Starland*.)

and now, as he waited for the eclipse to begin, he turned to a lad who stood behind him, almost hidden in the dark shadow—the one fortunate boy who had earned the right to share this night's work.

3

"We have still half an hour, Alwyn," said he, "before the eclipse will begin, and I can show you the moon's face well to-night.   Take my place here and look at her while I point out the chief features. See first, there are the grey plains (A, C, G, etc.) lying chiefly in the lower half of the moon.   You can often see these on a clear night with the naked eye, but you must remember that then they appear more in the upper part, because in the telescope we see the moon's face inverted or upside down.

"These plains were once thought to be oceans, but are now proved to be dry flat regions situated at different levels on the moon and much like what deserts and prairies would appear on our earth if seen from the same distance.   Looking through the telescope, is it not difficult to imagine how people could ever have pictured them as a man's face ?   But not so difficult to understand how some ancient nations thought the moon was a kind of mirror, in which our earth was reflected as in a looking-glass, with its seas and rivers, mountains and valleys ; for it does look something like a distant earth, and as the light upon it is really reflected from the sun it was very natural to compare it to a looking-glass.

"Next cast your eye over the hundreds of craters, some large, others quite small, which cover the moon's face with pitted marks, like a man with small-pox ; while a few of the larger rings look like holes made in a window-pane, where a stone has passed through, for brilliant shining streaks radiate from them on all sides like the rays of a star, covering a large part of the moon.   Brightest of all these starred craters is Tycho, which you will easily find near the top of the moon (1, Fig. 3), for you have often seen it in the small telescope. How grand it looks to-night in the full moon (Fig. 3*a*)! It is true you see all the craters better when the moon is in her quarters, because the light falls sideways upon them and the shadows are more sharply defined ; yet even at the full the bright ray of light on Tycho's rim marks out the huge cavity, and you can even see faintly the magnificent terraces which run round the cup within, one below the other.

"This cavity measures fifty-four miles across,

Fig. 4.

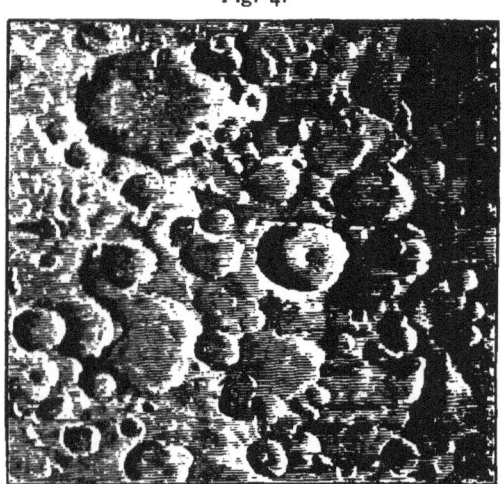

Tycho and his surroundings.
(From a photograph of the moon taken by Mr. De la Rue, 1863.)

so that if it could be moved down to our earth it would cover by far the largest part of Devon-shire, or that portion from Bideford on the north, to the sea on the south, and from the borders of Cornwall on the east, to Exeter on the west, and it is 17,000 feet or nearly three miles in depth. Even in the brilliant light of the full moon this enormous cup is dark compared to the bright rim, but it is much better seen in about the middle of the second quarter, when the rising sun begins to light up one side while the other is in black night. The drawing on the wall (Fig. 4), which is taken from an actual photograph of the moon's face, shows Tycho at this time surrounded by the numerous other craters which cover this part of the moon. You may recognise him by the gleaming peak in the centre of the cup, and by his bright rim which is so much more perfect than those of his companions. The gleaming peak is the top of a steep cone or hill rising up 6000 feet, or more than a mile from the base of the crater, so that even the summit is about two miles below the rim.

" There is one very interesting point in Tycho, however, which is seen at its very best at full moon. Look outside the bright rim and you will see that from the shadow which surrounds it there spring on all sides those strange brilliant streaks (see Fig. 3*a*) which I spoke of just now. There are others quite as bright, or even brighter, round other craters, Copernicus (Fig. 6), Kepler, and Aristarchus, lower down on the right-hand side of the moon ; but these of Tycho are far the most widely spread, covering almost all the top of the face.

" What are these streaks ?   We do not know. During the second quarter of the moon, when the sun is rising slowly upon Tycho, lighting up his peak and showing the crater beautifully divided into a bright cup in the curve to the right, while a dense shadow lies in the left hollow, these streaks are only faint, and among the many craters around (see Fig. 4) you might even have some difficulty at first in finding the well-known giant. But as the sun rises higher and higher they begin to appear, and go on increasing in brightness till they shine with that wonderfully silvery light you see now in the full moon.

Fig. 5.

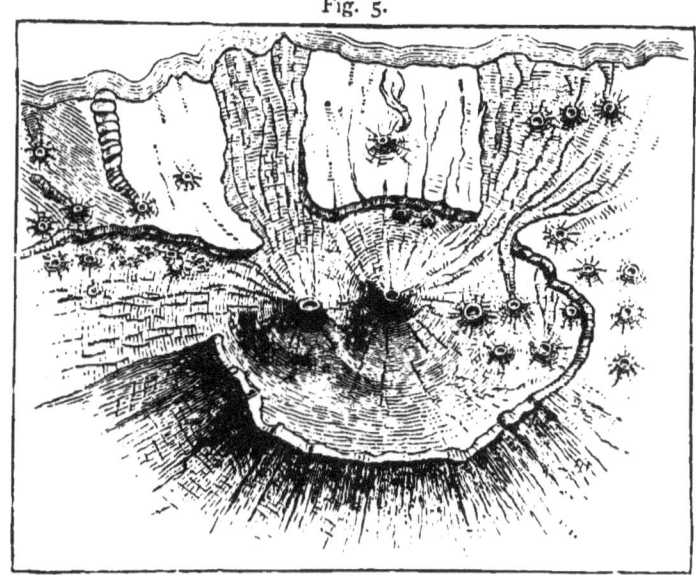

Plan of the Peak of Teneriffe, showing how it resembles
a lunar crater. (A. Geikie.)

" Here is a problem for you young astronomers to solve, as we learn more and more how to use the telescope with all its new appliances.

The crater itself is not so difficult to explain, for we have many like it on our earth, only not nearly so large.   In fact, we might almost say that our earthly volcanoes differ from those in the moon only by their smaller size and by forming *mountains* with the crater or cup on the top ; while the lunar craters lie flat on the surface of the moon, the hollow of the cup forming a depression below it.   The peak of Teneriffe (Fig. 5), which is a dormant volcano, is a good copy in minia-ture on our earth of many craters on the moon   The large plain surrounded by a high rocky wall, broken in places by lava streams, the smaller craters nestling in the cup, and the high peak or central crater rising up far above the others, are so like what we see on the moon that we cannot doubt that the same causes have been at work in both cases, even though the space enclosed in the rocky wall of Teneriffe measures only eight miles across, while that of Tycho measures fifty-four.

"But of the streaks we have no satisfactory expla-nation.   They pass alike over plain and valley and mountain, cutting even across other craters with-out swerving from their course.   The astronomer Nasmyth thought they were the remains of cracks made when the volcanoes were active, and filled with molten lava from below, as water oozes up through ice-cracks on a pond.   But this explana-tion is not quite satisfactory, for the lava, forcing its way through, would cool in ridges which ought to cast a shadow in sunlight.   These streaks, however, not only cast no shadow, as you can see at the full moon but when the sun shines sideways upon them

in the new or waning moon they disappear as we
have seen altogether.   Thus the streaks, so brilliant
at full moon in Tycho, Copernicus, Kepler, and
Aristarchus, remain a puzzle to astronomers still.

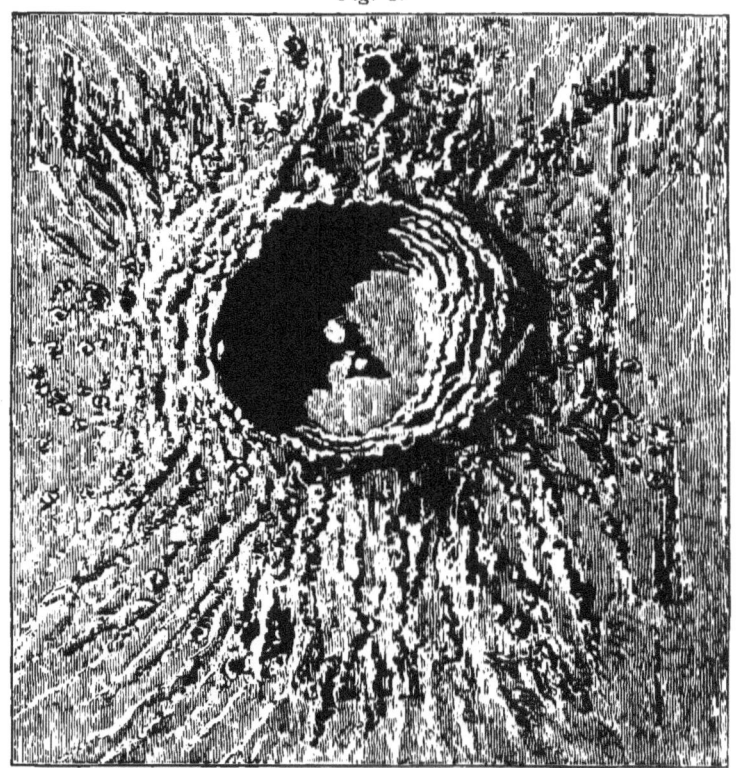

The crater Copernicus.
(As given in Herschel's *Astronomy*, from a drawing taken in a
reflecting telescope of 20 feet focal length.)

" We cannot examine these three last-named craters
well to-night with the full sun upon them ; but mark
their positions well, for Copernicus, at least, you must

examine on the first opportunity, when the sun is
rising upon it in the moon's second quarter. It is
larger even than Tycho, measuring fifty-six miles
across, and has a hill in the centre with many peaks;
while outside, great spurs or ridges stretch in all
directions sometimes for more than a hundred miles,
and between these are scattered innumerable minute
craters. But the most striking feature in it is the
ring, which is composed inside the crater of magnificent terraces divided by deep ravines. These
terraces are in some ways very like those of the
great crater of Teneriffe, and astronomers can best
account for them by supposing that this immense
crater was once filled with a lake of molten lava
rising, cooling at the edges, and then falling again,
leaving the solid ridge behind. The streaks are
also beautifully shown in Copernicus (see Fig. 6),
but, as in Tycho, they fade away as the sun sets
on the crater, and only reappear gradually as mid-
day approaches.

" And now, looking a little to the left of Copernicus,
you will see that grand range of mountains, the
Lunar Apennines (Fig. 7), which stretches 400 miles
across the face of the moon. Other mountain
ranges we could find, but none so like mountains
on our own globe as these, with their gentle sunny
slope down to a plain on the left, and steep
perpendicular cliffs on the right. The highest
peak in this range, called Huyghens, rises to the
height of 21,000 feet, higher than Chimborazo in
the Andes. Other mountains on the moon, such as
those called the Caucasus, south of the Apennines,

are composed of disconnected peaks, while others again stand as solitary pyramids upon the plains.

" But we must hasten on, for I want you to observe those huge walled crater-plains which have no hill

Fig. 7.

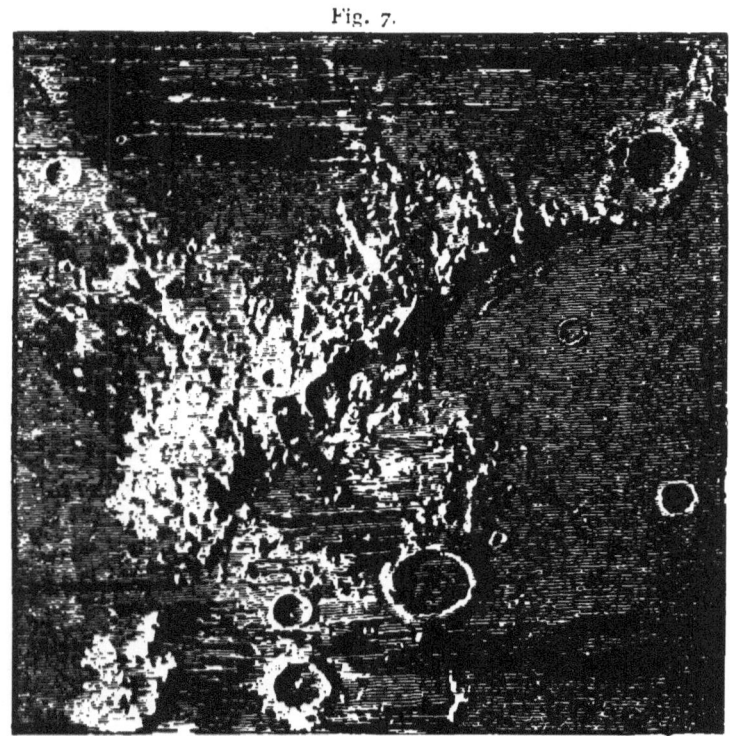

The Lunar Apennines.

(Copied by kind permission of MM. Henri from part of a magnificent photograph taken by them, March 29, 1890, at the Paris Observatory.)

in the middle, but smooth steel-grey centres shining like mirrors in the moonlight. One of these, called Archimedes, you will find just below the Lunar Apennines (Figs. 3 and 7), and another called Plato, which is sixty miles broad, is still lower down the

moon's face (Figs. 3 and 8). The centres of these broad
circles are curiously smooth and shining like quick-

Fig. 8.

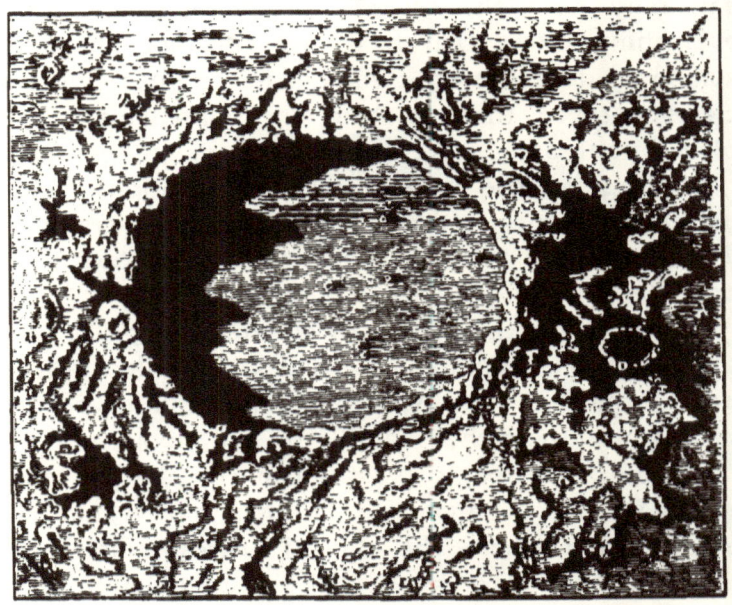

The crater Plato as seen soon after sunrise.   (After Neison.)

silver, with minute dots here and there which are
miniature craters, while the walls are rugged and
crowned with turret-shaped peaks.

"It is easy to picture to oneself how these may
once have been vast seas of lava, not surging as
in Copernicus, and heaving up as it cooled into
one great central cone, but seething as molten lead
does in a crucible, little bubbles bursting here and
there into minute craters ; and this is the explanation
given of them by astronomers.

" And now that you have seen the curious rugged face of the moon and its craters and mountains, you will want to know how all this has come about. We can only form theories on the point, except that everything shows that heat and volcanoes have in some way done the work, though no one has ever yet clearly proved that volcanic eruptions have taken place in our time. We must look back to ages long gone by for those mighty volcanic eruptions which hurled out stones and ashes from the great crater of Tycho, and formed the vast seas of lava in Copernicus and Plato.

."And when these were over, and the globe was cooling down rapidly, so that mountain ranges were formed by the wrinkling and rending of the surface, was there then any life on the moon? Who can tell? Our magic glasses can reveal what now is, so far as distance will allow ; but what has been, except where the rugged traces remain, we shall probably never know. What we now see is a dead worn-out planet, on which we cannot certainly trace any activity except that of heat in the past. That there is no life there now, at any rate of the kind on our own earth, we are almost certain ; first, because we can nowhere find traces of water, clouds, nor even mist, and without moisture no life like ours is possible ; and secondly, because even if there is, as perhaps there may be, a thin ocean of gas round the moon there is certainly no atmosphere such as surrounds our globe.

" One fact which proves this is, that there are no half-shadows on the moon. If you look some

night at the mountains and craters during her first
and second quarters, you will be startled to see what
heavy shadows they cast, not with faint edges dying
away into light, but sharp and hard (see Figs. 6-8),
so that you pass, as it were by one step, from shadow
to sunshine.   This in itself is enough to show that
there is no air to scatter the sunlight and spread it into
the edges of the shade as happens on our earth ; but
there are other and better proofs.   One of these is,
that during an eclipse of the sun there is no reflec-
tion of his light round the dark moon as there
would be if the moon had an atmosphere ; another is
that the spectroscope, that wonderful instrument
which shows us invisible gases, gives no hint of air
around the moon ; and another is the sudden dis-
appearance or *occultation* of a star behind the moon,
such as I hope to see in a few minutes.

" See here ! take the small hand telescope and turn
it on to the moon's face while I take my place at
the large one, and I will tell you what to look for.
You know that at sunset we see the sun for some
time after it has dipped below the horizon, because
the rays of light which come from it are bent in our
atmosphere and brought to our eyes, forming in
them the image of the sun which is already gone.
Now in a short time the moon which we are watching
will be darkened by our earth coming between it
and the sun, and while it is quite dark it will pass
over a little bright star.   In fact to us the star will
appear to set behind the dark moon as the sun sets
below the horizon, and if the moon had an atmosphere like ours, the rays from the star would be bent

in it and reach our eyes after the star was gone, so that it would only disappear gradually. Astronomers have always observed, however, that the star is lost to sight quite suddenly, showing that there is no ocean of air round the moon to bend the light-rays."

Here the magician paused, for a slight dimness on the lower right-hand side of the moon warned him that she was entering into the *penumbra* or

Fig. 9.

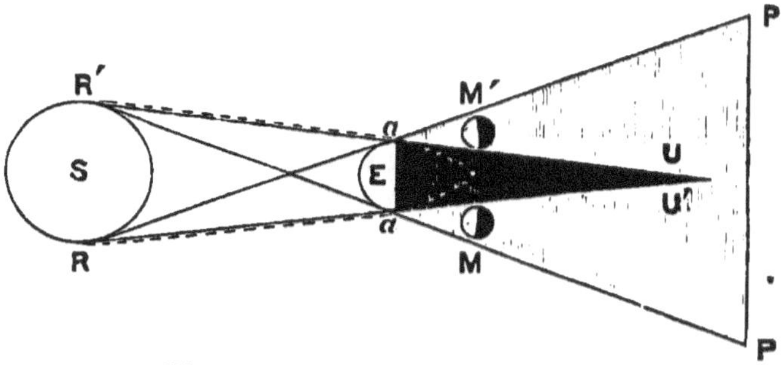

Diagram of total eclipse of the moon.

S, Sun.   E, Earth.   M, Moon passing into the earth's shadow and passing out at M'.

R, R', Lines meeting at a point U, U' behind the earth and enclosing a space within which all the direct rays of the sun are intercepted by the earth, causing a black darkness or *umbra*.

R, P and R', P', Lines marking a space within which, behind the earth, part of the sun's rays are cut off, causing a half-shadow or *penumbra*, P, P'.

a, a, Points where a few of the sun's rays are bent or refracted in the earth's atmosphere, so that they pass along the path marked by the dotted lines and shed a lurid light on the sun's face.

half-shadow (see Fig. 9) caused by the earth cutting off part of the sun's rays; and soon a deep black

4

shadow creeping over Aristarchus and Plato showed
that she was passing into that darker space or
umbra where the body of the earth is completely
between her and the sun and cuts off all his rays.
All, did I say? No! not all. For now was seen a
beautiful sight, which would prove to any one who
saw our earth from a great distance that it has a
deep ocean of air round it.

It was a clear night, with a cloudless sky, and
as the deep shadow crept slowly over the moon's
face, covering the Lunar Apennines and Copernicus,
and stealing gradually across the brilliant streaks of
Tycho till the crater itself was swallowed up in darkness, a strange lurid light began to appear. The
part of the moon which was eclipsed was not wholly
dark, but tinted with a very faint bluish-green light,
which changed almost imperceptibly, as the eclipse
went on, to rose-red, and then to a fiery copper-
coloured glow as the moon crept entirely into the
shadow and became all dark. The lad watching
through his small telescope noted this weird light, and
wondered, as he saw the outlines of the Apennines
and of several craters dimly visible by it, though
the moon was totally eclipsed. He noted, but was
silent. He would not disturb the Principal, for the
important moment was at hand, as this dark copper-
coloured moon, now almost invisible, drew near to
the star over which it was to pass.

This little star, really a glorious sun billions of miles
away behind the moon, was perhaps the centre of
another system of worlds as unknown to us as we to
them, and the fact of our tiny moon crossing between

it and our earth would matter as little as if a grain of sand was blown across the heavens. Yet to the watchers it was a great matter—would the star give any further clue to the question of an atmosphere round the moon ? Would its light linger even for a moment, like the light of the setting sun ? Nearer and nearer came the dark moon ; the star shone brilliantly against its darkness ; one second and it was gone. The long looked-for moment had passed, and the magician turned from his instrument with a sigh. " I have learnt nothing new, Alwyn," said he, " but at least it is satisfactory to have seen for ourselves the proof that there is no perceptible atmosphere round the moon. We need wait no longer, for before the star reappears on the other side the eclipse will be passing away."

" But, master," burst forth the lad, now the silence was broken, " tell me why did that strange light of many tints shine upon the dark moon ? "

" Did you notice it, Alwyn ? " said the Principal, with a pleased smile. " Then our evening's work is not lost, for you have made a real observation for yourself. That light was caused by the few rays of the sun which grazed the edge of our earth passing through the ocean of air round it (see Fig. 9). There they were refracted or bent, and so were thrown within the shadow cast by our earth, and fell upon the moon. If there were such a person as a ' man in the moon,' that lurid light would prove to him that our earth has an atmosphere. The cause of the tints is the same which gives us our sunset colours, because as the different coloured waves which make white light are absorbed one by one, passing through the denser atmosphere, the blue are cut off first, then the green, then the yellow, till only the orange and red rays reached the centre of the shadow, where the moon was darkest. But this is too difficult a subject to begin at midnight."

So saying, he lighted his lamp, and covering the object-glass of his telescope with its pasteboard cap, detached the instrument from the clockwork, and the master and his pupil went down the turret stairs and past through the room below. As they did so they heard in the distance a scuffling noise like that of rats in the wall. A smile passed over the face of the Principal, for he knew that his young pupils, who had been making their observations in the gallery above, were hurrying back to their beds.

CHAPTER II

MAGIC GLASSES, AND HOW TO USE THEM

HE sun shone brightly into the science class-room at mid-day. No gaunt shadows nor ghostly moonlight now threw a spell on the magic chamber above. The instruments looked bright and business-like, and the Principal, moving amongst them, heard the subdued hum of fifty or more voices rising from below. It was the lecture hour, and the subject for the day was, "Magic glasses, and how to use them." As the large clock in the hall sounded twelve, the Principal gathered up a few stray lenses and prisms he had selected, and passed down the turret stair to his platform. Behind him were arranged his diagrams, before him on the table stood various instruments, and the rows of bright faces beyond looked up with one consent as the hum quieted down and he began his lecture.

"I have often told you, boys, have I not? that I am a Magician. In my chamber near the sky I work spells as did the magicians of old, and by the help of my magic glasses I peer into the secrets of nature. Thus I read the secrets of the distant stars; I catch the light of wandering comets, and make it reveal its origin; I penetrate into the whirlpools of the sun; I map out the craters of the moon. Nor can the tiniest being on earth hide itself from me. Where others see only a drop of muddy water, that water brought into my magic chamber teems with thousands of active bodies, darting here and whirling there amid a meadow of tiny green plants floating in the water. Nay, my inquisitive glass sees even farther than this, for with it I can watch the eddies of water and green atoms going on in each of these tiny beings as they feed and grow. Again, if I want to break into the secrets of the rock at my feet, I have only to put a thin slice of it under my microscope to trace every crystal and grain; or, if I wish to learn still more, I subject it to fiery heat, and through the magic prisms of my spectroscope I read the history of the very substances of which it is composed. If I wish to study the treasures of the wide ocean, the slime from a rock-pool teems with fairy forms darting about in the live box imprisoned in a crystal home. If some distant stars are invisible even in the giant glasses of my telescope, I set another power to work, and make them print their own image on a photographic plate and so reveal their presence.

"All these things you have seen through my magic

glasses, and I promised you that one day I would explain to you how they work and do my bidding. But I must warn you that you must give all your attention ; there is no royal road to my magician's power. Every one can attain to it, but only by taking trouble. You must open your eyes and ears, and use your intelligence to test carefully what your senses show you.

" We have only to consider a little to see that we depend entirely upon our senses for our knowledge of the outside world. All kinds of things are going on around us, about which we know nothing, because our eyes are not keen enough to see, and our ears not sharp enough to hear them. Most of all we enjoy and study nature through our eyes, those windows which let in to us the light of heaven, and with it the lovely sights and scenes of earth ; and which are no ordinary windows, but most wonderful structures adapted for conveying images to the brain. They are of very different power in different people, so that a long-sighted person sees a lovely land-scape where a short-sighted one sees only a confused mist ; while a short-sighted person can see minute things close to the eye better than a long-sighted one.

" Let us try to understand this before we go on to artificial glasses, for it will help us to explain how these glasses show us many things we could never see without them. Here are two pictures of the human eyeball (Figs. 10 and 11), one as it appears from the front, and the other as we should see the parts if we cut an eyeball across from the front to

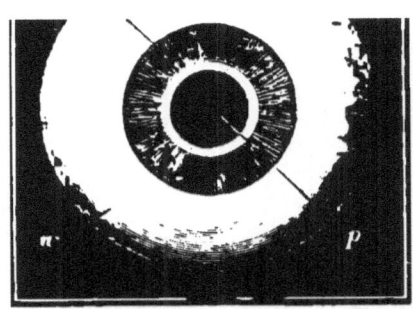

Eye-ball seen from the front.
After Le Gros Clark
w, White of eye. *i*, Iris. *p*, Pupil.

and a dark glassy mound *c. c* in the centre of the white in front. In this mound we can easily distinguish two parts—first, the coloured *iris* or elastic curtain (*i*, Fig. 10); and secondly, the dark spot or pupil *p* in the centre. The iris is the part which gives the eye its colour; it is composed of a number of fibres, the outer ones radiating towards the centre, the inner ones forming a ring round the pupil; and behind these fibres is a coat of dark pigment or colouring matter, blue in some people, grey, brown, or black in others. When the light is very strong, and would pain the nerves inside if too much entered the pupil or window of the eye, then the ring of the iris contracts so as partly to close the opening. When there is very little light, and it is necessary to let in as much as possible, the ring expands and the pupil grows large. The best way to observe this is to look at a cat's eyes in the dusk, and then bring her near to a bright light; for

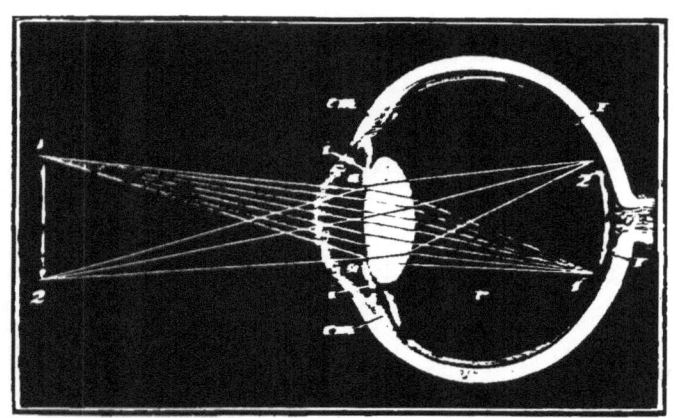

convex surfaces like an ordinary magnifying glass. This lens rests on a cushion of a soft jelly-like substance *v*, called the vitreous humour, which fills the dark chamber or cavity of the eyeball and keeps it in shape, so that the retina *r*, which lines the chamber, is kept at a proper distance from the lens. This retina is a transparent film of very sensitive nerves ; it forms a screen at the back of the chamber, and has a coating of very dark pigment or colouring matter behind it. Lastly, the nerves of the retina all meet in a bundle, called the optic nerve, and passing out of the eyeball at a point *on*, go to the brain. These are the chief parts we use in seeing ; now how do we use them ?

"Suppose that a pencil is held in front of the eye at the distance at which we see small objects comfortably. Light is reflected from all parts of the surface of the pencil, and as the rays spread, a certain number enter the pupil of the eye. We will follow only two cones of light coming from the points 1 and 2 on the diagram Fig. 11. These you see enter the eye, each widely spread over the cornea *c*. They are bent in a little by this curved covering, and by the liquid behind it, while the iris cuts off the rays near the edges of the lens, which would be too much bent to form a clear image. The rest of the rays fall upon the lens *l*. In passing through this lens they are very much bent (or *refracted*) towards each other, so much so that by the time they reach the end of the dark chamber *v*, each cone of light has come to a point or focus $1'$ $2'$, and as rays of this kind have come from every point all over the pencil, exactly similar points are formed on the retina, and a real picture of the pencil is formed there between 1′ and 2′.

" We will make a very simple and pretty experiment to illustrate this. Darkening the room I light a candle, take a square of white paper in my hand, and hold a simple magnifying glass between the two (see Fig. 12) about three inches away from the candle. Then I shift the paper nearer and farther behind the lens, till we get a clear image of the candle-flame

Fig. 12.

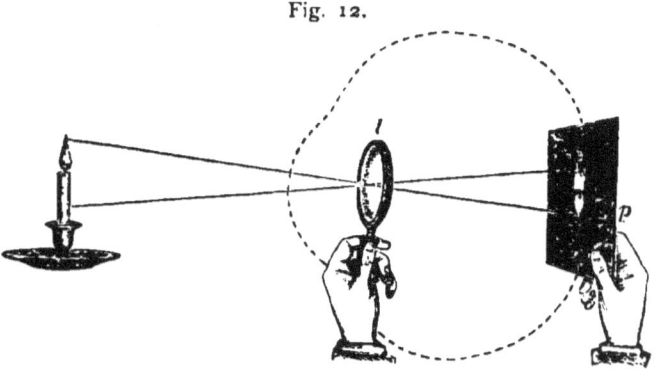

Image of a candle-flame thrown on paper by a lens.

upon it. This is exactly what happens in our eye. I have drawn a dotted line *c* round the lens and the paper on the diagram to represent the eyeball in which the image of the candle-flame would be on the retina instead of on the piece of paper. The first point you will notice is that the candle-flame is upside down on the paper, and if you turn back to Fig. 11 you will see why, for it is plain that the cones of light *cross* in the lens *l*, 1 going to 1′ and 2 to 2′. Every picture made on our retina is upside down.

" But it is not there that we see it. As soon as the points of light from the pencil strike upon the retina, the thrill passes on along the optic nerve *on*, through the back of the eye to the brain ; and our mind, following back the rays exactly as they have come through the lens, sees a pencil, outside the eye, right way upwards.

" This is how we see with our eyes, which adjust themselves most beautifully to our needs.   For example, not only is the iris always ready to expand or contract according as we need more or less light, but there is a special muscle, called the ciliary muscle (*cm*, Fig. 11), which alters the lens for us to see things far or near.   In all, or nearly all, perfect eyes the lens is flatter in front than behind, and this enables us to see things far off by bringing the rays from them exactly to a focus on the retina.   But when we look at nearer things the rays require to be more bent or refracted, so without any conscious effort on our part this ciliary muscle contracts and allows the lens to bulge out slightly in front.   Instantly we have a stronger magnifier, and the rays are brought to the right focus on the retina, so that a clear and full-size image of the near object is formed.   How little we think, as we turn our eyes from one thing to another, and observe, now the distant hills, now the sheep feeding close by ; or, as night draws on, gaze into limitless space and see the stars millions upon millions of miles away, that at every moment the focus of our eye is altering, the iris is contracting or expanding, and myriads of images are being formed one after the other in that little dark chamber, through which pass all the scenes of the outer world !

" Yet even this wonderful eye cannot show us every-thing. Some see farther than others, some see more minutely than others, according as the lens of the eye is flatter in one person and more rounded in another. But the most long-sighted person could never have discovered the planet Neptune, more than 2700 millions of miles distant from us, nor could the keenest-sighted have known of the existence of those minute and beautiful little plants, called diatoms, which live around us wherever water is found, and form delicate flint skeletons so infinitesimally small that thousands of millions go to form one cubic inch of the stone called tripoli, found at Bilin in Bohemia.

" It is here that our ' magic glasses ' come to our assistance, and reveal to us what was before invisible.

Fig. 13.

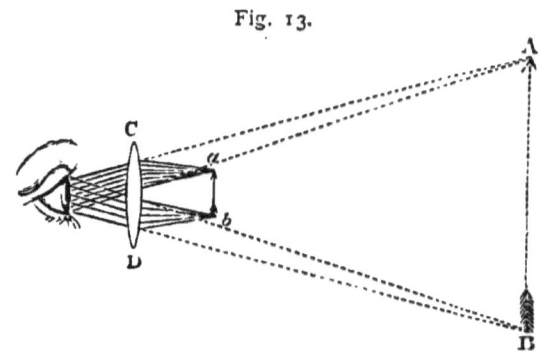

Arrow magnified by a convex lens.
a, b, Real arrow.   C, D, Magnifying-glass.   A, B, Enlarged image of the arrow.

We learnt just now that we see near things by the lens of our eye becoming more rounded in front ; but

5

there comes a point beyond which the lens cannot
bulge any more, so that when a thing is very tiny,
and would have to be held very close to the eye for
us to see it, the lens can no longer collect the rays
to a focus, so we see nothing but a blur.   More than
800 years ago an Arabian, named Alhazen, explained
why rounded or convex glasses make things appear
larger when placed before the eye.   This glass which

Fig. 14.

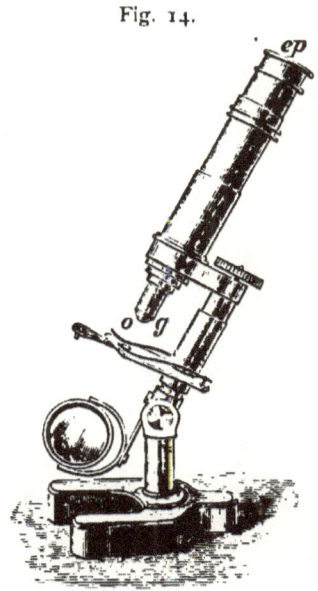

I hold in my hand is a simple
magnifying-glass, such as we
used for focusing the candle-
flame.   It bends the rays inwards from any small object
(see the arrow *a*, *b*, Fig. 13) so
that the lens of our eye can
use them, and then, as we
follow out the rays in straight
lines to the place where we
see clearly (at A, B), every
point of the object is magnified, and we not only see it
much larger, but every mark
upon it is much more distinct.
You all know how the little
shilling magnifying - glasses
you carry show the most
lovely and delicate structures
in flowers, on the wings of

Student's microscope.
ep, Eye-piece. *o, g*, Object-
glass.

butterflies, on the head of a bee or fly, and, in fact,
in all minute living things.

"But this is only our first step.   Those diatoms we
spoke of just now will only look like minute specks

under even the strongest magnifying-glass. So we pass on to use two extra lenses to assist our eyes, and come to this compound microscope (Fig. 14) through which I have before now shown you the delicate markings on shells which were themselves so minute that you could not see them with the naked eye. Now we have to discover how the microscope performs this feat. Going back again for a minute to our candle and magnifying-glass (Fig. 12), you will find that the nearer you put the lens to the candle the farther away you will have to put the paper to get a clear image. When in a microscope we put a powerful lens *o, l* close down to a very minute object, say a spicule of a flint sponge *s, s*, quite invisible to the unaided eye, the rays from this spicule are brought to a focus a long way behind it at *s′, s′*, making an enlarged image

Fig. 15.

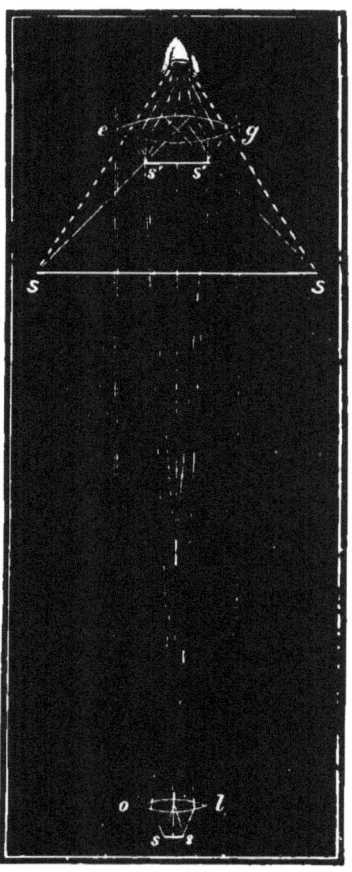

Skeleton of a microscope, showing how an object is magnified. *o, l,* Object-lens. *e, g,* Eye-glass. *s, s,* Spicule. *s′, s′,* Magnified image of same in the tube. S, S, Image again enlarged by the lens of the eye-piece.

because the lines of light have been diverging ever since they crossed in the lens. If you could put a piece of paper at s' s', as you did in the candle experiment, you would see the actual image of the magnified spicule upon it. But as these points of light are only in an empty tube, they pass on, spreading out again from the image, as they did before from the spicule. Then another convex lens or eye-glass e, g is put at the top of the microscope at the proper distance to bend these rays so that they enter our eye in nearly parallel lines, exactly as we saw in the ordinary magnifying-glass (Fig. 13), and our crystalline lens can then bring them to a focus on our retina.

" By this time the spicule has been twice magnified ; or, in other words, the rays of light coming from it have been twice bent towards each other, so that when our eye follows them out in straight lines they are widely spread, and we see every point of light so clearly that all the spots and markings on this minute spicule are as clear as if it were really as large as it looks to us.

" This is simply the principle of the microscope. When you come to look at your own instruments, though they are very ordinary ones, you will find that the object-glass o, l is made of three lenses, flat on the side nearest the tube, and each lens is composed of two kinds of glass in order to correct the unequal refraction of the rays, and prevent fringes of colour appearing at the edge of the lens. Then again the eye-piece will be a short tube with a lens at each end, and halfway between them a black ledge will be seen inside the tube which acts like the iris of our eye (*i*, Fig. 11) and cuts off the rays passing through the edges of the lens. All these are devices to correct faults in the microscope which our eye corrects for itself, and they have enabled opticians to make very powerful lenses.

"Look now at the diagram (Fig. 16) showing a group of diatoms which you can see under the microscope after the lecture. Notice the lovely patterns, the delicate tracery, and the fine lines on the diatoms shown there. Yet each of these minute flint skeletons, if laid on a piece of glass by itself, would be quite invisible to the naked eye, while hundreds of them together only look like a faint mist on the slide on which they lie. Nor are they even here shown as much magnified as they might be; under a stronger power we should see those delicate lines on the diatoms broken up into minute round cups.

Fig. 16.

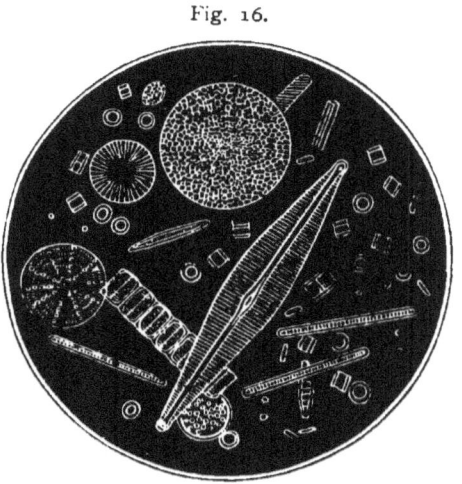

Fossil diatoms seen under the microscope. The largest of these is an almost imperceptible speck to the naked eye.

"Is it not wonderful and delightful to think that we are able to add in this way to the power of our eyes, till it seems as if there were no limit to the hidden beauties of the minute forms of our earth, if only we can discover them?

" But our globe does not stand alone in the universe, and we want not only to learn all about everything we find upon it, but also to look out into the vast space around us and discover as much as we can about the myriads of suns and planets, comets and meteorites, star-mists and nebulæ, which are to be found there. Even with the naked eye we can admire the grand planet Saturn, which is more than 800 millions of miles away, and this in itself is very marvellous. Who would have thought that our tiny crystalline lens would be able to catch and focus rays, sent all this enormous distance, so as actually to make a picture on our retina of a planet, which, like the moon, is only sending back to us the light of the sun? For, remember, the rays which come to us from Saturn must have travelled twice 800 millions of miles—884 millions from the sun to the planet, and less or more from the planet back to us, according to our position at the time. But this is as nothing when compared to the enormous distances over which light travels from the stars to us. Even the nearest star we know of, is at least twenty *millions* of *millions* of miles away, and the light from it, though travelling at the rate of 186,300 miles in a second, takes four years and four months to reach us, while the light from others, which we can see without a telescope, is between twenty and thirty years on its road. Does not the thought fill us with awe, that our little eye should be able to span such vast distances?

" But we are not yet nearly at the end of our

wonder, for the same power which devised our eye gave us also the mind capable of inventing an instrument which increases the strength of that eye till we can actually see stars so far off that their light takes *two thousand years* coming to our globe. If the microscope delights us in helping us to see things invisible without it, because they are so small, surely the telescope is fascinating beyond all other magic glasses when we think that it brings heavenly bodies, thousands of billions of miles away, so close to us that we can examine them.

"A Telescope (Fig. 17) can, like the microscope, be made of only two glasses : an object-glass to form an image in the tube and a magnifying eye-piece to enlarge it. But there is this difference, that the object lens of a microscope is put close down to a minute object, so that the rays fall upon it at a wide angle, and the image formed in the tube is very much larger than the object outside. In the telescope, on the contrary, the thing we look at is far off, so that the rays fall on the object-glass at such a

Fig. 17.

An astronomical telescope.
e, Eye-piece. *og*, Object-glass.
f, Finder.

very narrow angle as to be practically parallel, and the image in the tube is of course *very*, *very* much smaller than the house, or church, or planet it pictures. What the object-glass of the telescope does for us, is to bring a small *real image* of an object very far off close to us in the tube of the telescope so that we can examine it.

"Think for a moment what this means. Imagine that star we spoke of (p. 41), whose light, travelling 186,300 miles in one second, still takes 2000 years to reach us. Picture the tiny waves of light crossing the countless billions of miles of space during those two thousand years, and reaching us so widely spread out that the few faint rays which strike our eye are quite useless, and for us that star has no existence ; we cannot see it. Then go and ask the giant telescope, by turning the object-glass in the direction where that star lies in infinite space. The widespread rays are collected and come to a minute bright image in the dark tube. You put the eye-piece to this image, and there, under your eye, is a shining point : this is the image of the star, which otherwise would be lost to you in the mighty distance.

"Can any magic tale be more marvellous, or any thought grander, or more sublime than this? From my little chamber, by making use of the laws of light, which are the same wherever we turn, we can penetrate into depths so vast that we are not able even to measure them, and bring back unseen stars to tell us the secrets of the mighty universe. As far as the stars are concerned, whether we see them or not depends entirely upon the number of rays collected by the object-glass ; for at such enormous distances the rays have no angle that we can measure, and magnify as you will, the brightest star only remains a point of light. It is in order to collect enough rays that astronomers have tried to have larger and larger object-glasses ; so that while a small good hand telescope, such as you use, may have an object-glass measuring only an inch and a quarter across, some of the giant telescopes have lenses of two and a half feet, or thirty inches, diameter. These enormous lenses are very difficult to make and manage, and have many faults, therefore astronomical telescopes are often made with curved mirrors to *reflect* the rays, and bring them to a focus instead of *refracting* them as curved lenses do.

"We see, then, that one very important use of the telescope is to bring objects into view which otherwise we would never see ; for, as I have already said, though we bring the stars into sight, we cannot magnify them. But whenever an object is near enough for the rays to fall even at a very small perceptible angle on the object-glass, then we can magnify them ; and the longer the telescope, and the stronger the eye-piece, the more the object is magnified.

"I want you to understand the meaning of this, for it is really very simple, only it requires a little thought. Here are skeleton drawings of two telescopes (Fig. 18), one double the length of the other. Let us suppose that two people are using them to look at an arrow on a weathercock a long distance off. The rays of light *r*, *r* from the two ends of the arrow will enter both telescopes at the same angle *r*, *x*, *r*, cross in the lens, and pass on at *exactly the same angle* into

Fig. 18.

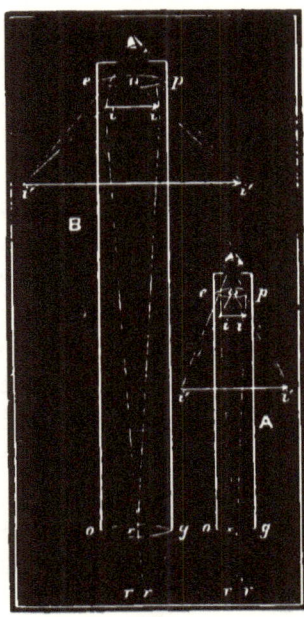

Skeletons of telescopes.

A, A one-foot telescope with a three-inch eye-piece. B, A two-foot telescope with a three-inch eye-piece. *e, p,* Eye-piece. *o, g,* Object-glass. *r, r,* Rays which enter the telescopes and crossing at *x* form an image at *i, i,* which is magnified by the lens *e, p.* The angles *r, x, r* and *i, x, i* are the same. In A the angle *i, o, i* is four times greater than that of *i, x, i.* In B it is eight times greater.

the tubes. So far all is alike, but now comes the difference. In the short telescope A the object-glass must be of such a curve as to bring the cones of light in each ray to a focus at a distance of *one foot* behind it,[1] and there a small image *i, i* of the arrow is formed. But B being twice the length, allows the lens to be less curved, and the image to be formed *two feet* behind the object-glass ; and as the rays *r, r* have been *diverging* ever since they crossed at *x,* the real image of the arrow formed at *i, i* is twice the size of the same image in A. Nevertheless, if you could put a piece of paper at *i, i* in both telescopes, and look through the *object-glass* (which you cannot actually do, because your head would block out the rays), the arrow would appear the same size in both telescopes, because one would be twice as far off from you as the other, and the angle *i, x, i* is the same in both.

---

[1] In our Fig. 18 the distances are inches instead of feet, but the proportions are the same.

" But by going to the proper end of the telescope you can get quite near the image, and can see and magnify it, if you put a strong lens to collect the rays from it to a focus.   This is the use of the eye-piece, which in our diagram is placed at a quarter of a foot or three inches from the image in both tele-scopes.   Now that we are close to the images, the divergence of the points i, i makes a great difference. In the small telescope, in which the image is only *one foot* behind the object-glass, the eye-piece being a quarter of a foot from it, is four times nearer, so the angle i, o, i is four times the angle i, x, i, and the man looking through it sees the image magnified *four times.*   But in the longer telescope the image is *two feet* behind the lens, while the eye-piece is, as before, a quarter of a foot from it.   Thus the eye-piece is now eight times nearer, so the angle i, o, i is eight times the angle i, x, i, and the observer sees the image magnified *eight times.*

" In real telescopes, where the difference between the focal length of the object-glass and that of the eye-glass can be made enormously greater, the magnifying power is quite startling, only the object-glass must be large, so as to collect enough rays to bear spreading widely.   Even in your small tele-scopes, with a focus of eighteen inches, and an object-glass measuring one and a quarter inch across, we can put on a quarter of an inch eye-piece, and so magnify seventy-two times ; while in my observatory telescope, eight feet or ninety-six inches long, an eye-piece of half an inch magnifies 192 times, and I can put on a $\frac{1}{8}$-inch eye-piece and magnify 768 times! And so we can go on lengthening the focus of the object-glass and shortening the focus of the eye-piece, till in Lord Rosse's gigantic fifty-six-foot telescope, in which the image is fifty-four feet (648 inches) behind the object-glass, an eye-piece one-eighth of an inch from the image magnifies 5184 times! These giant telescopes, however, require an enormous object-glass or mirror, for the points of light are so spread out in making the large image that it is very faint unless an enormous number of rays are collected. Lord Rosse's telescope has a reflecting mirror measuring six feet across, and a man can walk upright in the telescope tube. The most powerful telescope yet made is that at the Lick Observatory, on Mount Hamilton, in California. It is fifty-six and a half feet long, the object-lens measures thirty-six inches across. A star seen through this telescope appears 2000 times as bright as when seen with the naked eye.

"You need not, however, wait for an opportunity to look through giant telescopes, for my small student's telescope, only four feet long, which we carry out on to the lawn, will show you endless unseen wonders; while your hand telescopes, and even a common opera-glass, will show many features on the face of the moon, and enable you to see the crescent of Venus, Jupiter's moons, and Saturn's rings, besides hundreds of stars unseen by the naked eye.

"Of course you will understand that Fig. 18 only shows the *principle* of the telescope. In all good instruments the lenses and other parts are more complicated ; and in a terrestrial telescope, for looking at objects on the earth, another lens has to be put in to turn them right way up again. In looking at the sky it does not matter which way up we see a planet or a star, so the second glass is not needed, and we lose light by using it.

"We have now three magic glasses to work for us—the magnifying-glass, the microscope, and the telescope. Besides these, however, we have two other helpers, if possible even more wonderful. These are the Photographic camera and the Spectroscope.

"Now that we thoroughly understand the use of lenses, I need scarcely explain this photographic camera (Fig. 19), for it is clearly an artificial eye. In place of the *crystalline lens* (compare with Fig. 11) the photographer uses one, or generally two lenses *l, l*, with a black ledge or stop *s* between them, which acts like the iris in cutting off the rays too near the edge of the lens. The dark camera *c* answers to the *dark chamber* of the eyeball, and the plate *p, p* at the back of the chamber, which is made sensitive by chemicals, answers our *retina*. The box is formed of two parts, sliding one within the other at *c*, so as to place the plate at a proper distance

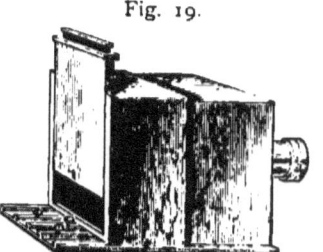

Fig. 19.

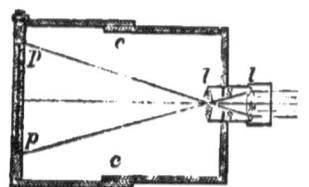

Photographic camera.

l, l, Lenses. *s, s,* Screen cutting off diverging rays. *c c,* Sliding box. *p, p,* Picture formed.

from the lens, and then a screw adjusts the focus more exactly by bringing the front lens back or forward, instead of altering the curve as the *ciliary muscle* does in our eye. The difference between the two instruments is that in our eye the message goes to the brain, and the image disappears when we turn our eyes away from the object; but in the camera the waves of light work upon the chemicals, and the image can be fixed and remain for ever.

" But the camera has at least one weak point. The screen at the back is not curved like our retina, but must be flat because of printing off the pictures, and therefore the parts of the photograph near the edge are a little out of proportion.

" In many ways, however, this photographic eye is a more faithful observer than our own, and helps us to make more accurate pictures. For instance, instantaneous photographs have been taken of a galloping horse, and we find that the movements are very different from what we thought we saw with our eye, because our retina does not throw off one impression after another quickly enough to be quite certain we see each curve truly in succession. Again, the photograph of a face gives minute curves and lines, lights and shadows, far more perfectly than even the best artist can see them, and when the picture is magnified we see more and more details which escaped us before.

" But it is especially when attached to the microscope or the telescope that the photographic apparatus tells us such marvellous secrets; giving us, for instance, an accurate picture of the most minute water-animal quite invisible to the naked eye, so that when we enlarge the photograph any one can see the beautiful markings, the finest fibre, or the tiniest granule ; or affording us accurate pictures, such as the one at p. 19 of the face of the moon, and bringing stars into view which we cannot otherwise see even with the strongest telescope.

"Our own eye has many weaknesses. For example, when we look through the telescope at the sky we can only fix our attention on one part at once, and afterwards on another ; and the picture which we see in this way, bit by bit, we must draw as best we can. But if we put a sensitive photographic plate into the telescope just at the point (*i, i*, Fig. 18), where the *image* of the sky is focused, this plate gives attention, so to speak, to the whole picture at once, and registers every point exactly as it is ; and this picture can be kept and enlarged so that every detail can be seen.

"Then, again, if we look at faint stars, they do not grow any brighter as we look. Each ray sends its message to the brain, and that is all ; we cannot heap them up in our eye, and, indeed, after a time we see less, because our nerves grow tired. But on a photographic plate in a telescope, each ray in its turn does a little work upon the chemicals, and the longer the plate remains, the stronger the picture becomes. When wet plates were used they could not be left long, but since dry plates have been invented, with a film of chemically prepared gelatine, they can be left for hours in the telescope, which is

kept by clockwork accurately opposite to the same
objects.   In this way thousands of faint stars, which
we cannot see with the strongest telescope, creep
into view as their feeble rays work over and over
again on the same spot ; and, as the brighter stars
as well as the faint ones are all the time making
their impression stronger, when the plate comes out
each one appears in its proper strength.   On the
other hand, very bright objects often become blurred
by a long exposure, so that we have sometimes to
sacrifice the clearness of a bright object in order to
print faint objects clearly.

    " We now come to our last magic glass—the
Spectroscope ; and the hour has slipped by so fast
that I have very little time left to speak of it.   But
this matters less as we have studied it before.[1]   I
need now only remind you of some of the facts.   You
will remember that when we passed sunlight through
a three-sided piece of glass called a prism, we broke
up a ray of white light into a line of beautiful
colours gradually passing from red, through orange,
yellow, green, blue, and indigo, to violet, and that
these follow in the same order as we see them in the
rainbow or in the thin film of a soap-bubble.   By
various experiments we proved that these colours are
separated from each other because the many waves
which make up white light are of different sizes, so
that because the waves of red light are slow and
heavy, they lag behind when bent in the three-sided
glass, while the rapid violet waves are bent more out

    [1] *Fairyland of Science,* Lecture II. ; and *Short History of Natural
Science,* chapter xxxiv.

of their road and run to the farther end of the line, the other colours ranging themselves between.

"Now when the light falls through the open window, or through a round hole or *large* slit, the images of the hole made by each coloured wave overlap each other very much, and the colours in the spectrum or coloured band are crowded together. But when in the spectroscope we pass the ray of light through a very narrow slit, each coloured image of the

Fig. 20.

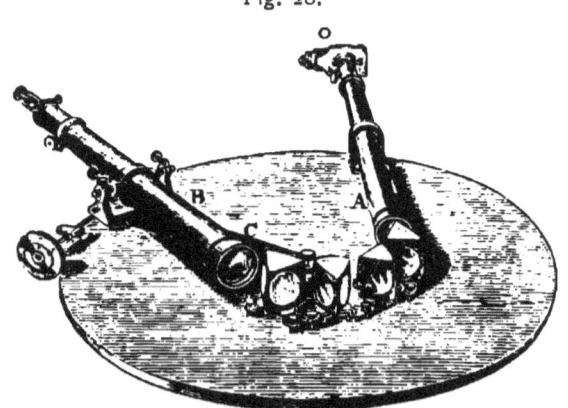

Kirchhoff's spectroscope.
A, The telescope which receives the ray of light
through the slit in O.

upright slit overlaps the next upright image only very little. By using several prisms one after the other (see Fig. 21), these upright coloured lines are separated more and more till we get a very long band or spectrum. Yet, as you know from our experiments with the light of a glowing wire or of molten iron, however much you spread out the light given by a solid or liquid, you can never separate these coloured lines from each other. It is only when you throw the light of a glowing gas or vapour into the slit that you get a few bright lines standing out alone. This is because *all* the rays of white light are present in glowing solids and liquids, and they follow each other too closely to be separated. But a gas, such as glowing hydrogen for example, gives out only a few separate rays, which, pouring through the slit, throw red, greenish-blue, and dark blue lines on the screen. Thus you have seen the double, orange-yellow sodium line (3, Plate I.) which starts out at once when salt is held in a flame and its light thrown into the spectroscope, and the red line of potassium vapour under the same treatment; and we shall observe these again when we study the coloured lights of the sun and stars.

Fig. 21.

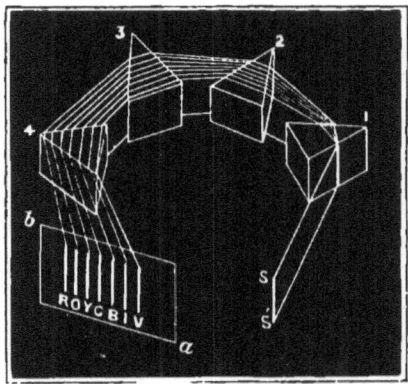

Passage of rays through the spectroscope. S, S', Slit through which the light falls on the prisms. 1, 2, 3, 4, Prisms in which the rays are dispersed more and more. *a, b*, Screen receiving the spectrum, of which the seven principal colours are marked.

"We see, then, that the work of our magic glass, the spectroscope, is simply to sift the waves of light, and that these waves, from their colour and their position in the long spectrum, actually tell us what glowing gases have started them on their road. Is not this like magic? I take a substance made of I know not what ; I break it up, and, melting it in the intense heat of an electric spark, throw its light into the spectroscope. Then, as I examine this light after it has been spread out by the prisms, I can actually read by unmistakable lines what metals or non-metals it contains. Nay, more ; when I catch the light of a star, or even of a faint nebula, in my telescope, and pass it through these prisms, there, written up on the magic-coloured band, I read off the gases which are glowing in that star-sun or star-dust billions of miles away.

"Now, boys, I have let you into the secrets of my five magic glasses—the magnifying-glass, the microscope, the telescope, the photographic camera, and the spectroscope. With these and the help of chemistry you can learn to work all my spells. You can peep into the mysteries of the life of the tiniest being which moves unseen under your feet ; you can peer into that vast universe, which we can never visit so long as our bodies hold us down to our little earth ; you can make the unseen stars print their spots of light on the paper you hold in your hand, by means of light-waves, which left them hundreds of years ago ; or you can sift this light in your spectroscope, and make it tell you what substances were glowing in that star when they were started on their road. All this you can do on one condition, namely, that you seek patiently to know the truth.

"Stories of days long gone by tell us of true magicians and false magicians, and the good or evil they wrought.   Of these I know nothing, but I do know this, that the value of the spells you can work with my magic glasses depends entirely upon whether you work patiently, accurately, and honestly.   If you make careless, inaccurate experiments, and draw hasty conclusions, you will only do bad work, which it may take others years to undo ; but if you question your instruments honestly and carefully, they will answer truly and faithfully.   You may make many mistakes, but one experiment will correct the other ; and while you are storing up in your own mind knowledge which lifts you far above this little world, or enables you to look deep below the outward surface of life, you may add your little group of facts to the general store, and help to pave the way to such grand discoveries as those of Newton in astronomy, Bunsen and Kirchhoff in spectrum analysis, and Darwin in the world of life."

CHAPTER III

FAIRY RINGS AND HOW THEY ARE MADE

IT was a lovely warm day in September, the golden corn had been cut and carted, and the waggons of the farmers around were free for the use of the college lads in their yearly autumn holiday. There they stood in a long row, one behind the other in the drive round the grounds, each with a pair of sleek, powerful farm-horses, and the waggoners beside them with their long whips ornamented with coloured ribbons : and as each waggon drew up before the door, it filled rapidly with its merry load and went on its way.

They had a long drive of seven miles before them, for they were going to cross the wild moor, and then descend gradually along a fairly good road to the more wooded and fertile country. Their object that day was to reach a certain fairy dell known to a few only among the party as one of the loveliest spots in Devon.   It was a perfect day for a picnic.   As they drove over the wide stretches of moorland, with tors to right and tors to the left, the stunted furze bushes growing here and there glistened with spiders' webs from which the dew had not yet disappeared, and mosses in great variety carpeted the ground, from the lovely thread-mosses, with their scarlet caps, to the pale sphagnum of the bogs, where a halt was made for some of the botanists of the party to search for the little Sundew (*Drosera rotundifolia*). Though this little plant had now almost ceased to flower, it was not difficult to recognise by its rosette of leaves glistening with sticky glands which it spreads out in many of the Dartmoor bogs to catch the tiny flies and suck out their life's blood, and several specimens were uprooted and carefully packed away to plant in moist moss at home.

From this bog onwards the road ran near by one of the lovely streams which feed the rivers below, and, passing across a bridge covered with ivy, led through a small forest of stunted trees round which the wood-bine clung, hanging down its crimson berries, and the bracken fern, already putting on its brown and yellow tints, grew tall and thick on either side.   Then, as they passed out of the wood, they came upon the dell, a piece of wild moorland lying in a hollow between two granite ridges, with large blocks of granite strewn over it here and there, and furze bushes growing under their shelter, still covered with yellow blossoms together with countless seed-bearing pods, which the youngsters soon gathered for the shiny black seeds within them.

Here the waggons were unspanned, the horses tethered out, the food unpacked, and preparations for the picnic soon in full swing. Just at this moment, however, a loud shout from one part of the dell called every one's attention. " The fairy rings ! the fairy rings ! we have found the fairy rings !" and there truly on the brown sward might be seen three delicate green rings, the fresh sprouting grass growing young and tender in perfect circles measuring from six feet to nearly three yards across.

" What are they ? " The question came from many voices at once, but it was the Principal who answered

" Why, do you not know that they are pixie circles, where the 'elves of hills, brooks, standing lakes, and groves ' hold their revels, whirling in giddy round, and making the rings, 'whereof the ewe not bites'? Have you forgotten how Mrs. Quickly, in the *Merry Wives of Windsor*, tells us that

> " ' nightly, meadow-fairies, look you sing,
> Like to the Garter's compass, in a ring :
> The expressure that it bears, green let it be,
> More fertile-fresh than all the field to see ' ?

" If we are magicians and work spells under magic glasses, why should not the pixies work spells on the grass ? I brought you here to-day on purpose to see them. Which of you now can name the pixie who makes them ? "

A deep silence followed. If any knew or guessed the truth of the matter, they were too shy to risk making a mistake.

"Be off with you then," said the Principal, "and keep well away from these rings all day, that you may not disturb the spell.   But come back to me before we return at night, and perhaps I may show you the wonder-working pixie, and we may take him home to examine under the microscope."

The day passed as such happy days do, and the glorious harvest moon had risen over the distant tors before the horses were spanned and the waggons ready.   But the Principal was not at the starting place, and looking round they saw him at the farther end of the dell.

"Gently, gently," he cried, as there was one general rush towards him ; "look where you tread, for I stand within a ring of fairies!"

And then they saw that just outside the green circle in which he stood, forming here and there a broken ring, were patches of a beautiful tiny mushroom, each of which raised its pale brown umbrella in the bright moonlight.

"Here are our fairies, boys.   I am going to take a few home where they can be spared from the ring, and to-morrow we will learn their history."

The following day saw the class-room full, and from the benches eager eyes were turned to the eight windows, in each of which stood one of the elder boys at his microscope ready for work.   For under those microscopes the Principal always arranged some object referred to in his lecture and figured in diagrams on the walls, and it was the duty of each boy, after the lecture was over, to show and explain to the class all the points of the specimen under his care. These boys were always specially envied, for though the others could, it is true, follow all the descriptions from the diagrams, yet these had the plant or animal always under their eye. Discussion was at this moment running high, for there was a great uncertainty of opinion as to whether a mushroom could be really called a plant when it had no leaves or flowers. All at once the hush came, as the Principal stepped into his desk and began :—

" Life is hard work, boys, and there is no being in this world which has not to work for its living. You all know that a plant grows by taking in gases and water, and working them up into sap and living tissue by the help of the sunshine and the green matter in their leaves ; and you know, too, that the world is so full of green plants that hundreds and thousands of young seedlings can never get a living, but are stifled in their babyhood or destroyed before they can grow up.

" Now there are many dark, dank places in the world where plants cannot get enough sunlight and air to make green colouring matter and manufacture their own food. And so it comes to pass that a certain class of plants have found another way of living, by taking their food ready made from other decaying plants and animals, and so avoiding the necessity of manufacturing it for themselves. These plants can live hidden away in dark cellars and damp cupboards, in drains and pipes where no light ever enters, under a thick covering of dead leaves in the forest, under fallen trunks and

7

mossy stones ; in fact, wherever decaying matter, whether of plant or animal, can be found for them to feed upon.

"It is to this class, called *fungi*, which includes all mushrooms and moulds, mildews, smuts, and ferments, that the mushroom belongs which we found yesterday making the fairy rings. And, in truth, we were not so far wrong when we called them pixies or imps, for many of them are indeed imps of mischief, which play sorry pranks in our stores at home and in the fields and forest abroad. They grow on our damp bread, or cheese, or pickles ; they destroy fruit and corn, hop and vine, and even take the life of insects and other animals. Yet, on the other hand, they are useful in clearing out unhealthy nooks and corners, and purifying the air ; and they can be made to do good work by those who know how to use them ; for without ferments we could have neither wine, beer, nor vinegar, nor even the yeast which lightens our bread.

"I am going to-day to introduce you to this large vagabond class of plants, that we may see how they live, grow, and spread, what good and bad work they do, and how they do it. And before we come to the mushrooms, which you know so well, we must look at the smaller forms, which do all their work above ground, so that we can observe them. For the *fungi* are to be found almost everywhere. The film growing over manure-heaps, the yeast plant, the wine fungus, and the vinegar plant ; the moulds and mildews covering our cellar-walls and cupboards, or growing on decayed leaves and wood, on stale fruit, bread, or jam, or making black spots on the leaves of the rose, the hop, or the vine ; the potato fungus, eating into the potato in the dark ground and producing disease ; the smut filling the grains of wheat and oats with disease, the ergot feeding on the rye, the rust which destroys beetroot, the rank toadstools and puff-balls, the mushroom we eat, and the truffles which form even their fruit underground,—all these are *fungi*, or lowly plants which have given up making their own food in the sunlight, and take it ready made from the dung, the decaying mould, the root, the leaf, the fruit, or the germ on which they grow. Lastly, the diseases which kill the silkworm and the common house-fly, and even some of the worst skin diseases in man, are caused by minute plants of this class feeding upon their hosts.

" In fact, the *fungi* are so widely spread over all things living and dead, that there is scarcely anything free from them in one shape or another. The

Fig. 22.

Three forms of vegetable mould magnified.
1, *Mucor Mucedo.* 2, *Aspergillus glaucus.* 3, *Penicillium glaucum*.

minute spores, now of one kind, now of another, float in the air, and settling down wherever they find suitable food, have nothing more to do than to feed, fatten, and increase, which they do with wonderful rapidity. Let us take as an example one of the moulds which covers damp leaves, and even the paste and jam in our cupboard. I have some here growing upon a basin of paste, and you see it forms a kind of dense white fur all over the surface, with here and there a bluish-green tinge upon it. This white fur is the common mould, *Mucor Mucedo* (1, Fig. 22), and the green mould happens in this case to be another mould, *Penicillium glaucum* (3, Fig. 22); but I must warn you that these minute moulds look very much alike until you examine them under the microscope, and though they are called white, blue, or green moulds, yet any one of them may be coloured at different times of its growth. Another very common and beautiful mould, *Aspergillus glaucus* (2, Fig. 22), often grows with Mucor on the top of jam.

"All these plants begin with a spore or minute colourless cell of living matter (*s*, Fig. 23), which spends its energy in sending out tubes in all directions into the leaves, fruit, or paste on which it feeds. The living matter, flowing now this way now that, lays down the walls of its tubes as it flows, and by and by, here and there, a tube, instead of working into the paste, grows upwards into the air and swells at the tip into a colourless ball in which a number of minute seed-like bodies called spores are formed. The ball bursts, the spores fall out, and each one begins to form fresh tubes, and so little by little the mould grows denser and thicker by new plants starting in all directions.

" Under the first microscope you will see a slide showing the tubes which spread through the paste, and which are called the *mycelium* (*m*, Fig. 23), and amongst it are three upright tubes, one just starting *a*, another with the fruit ball forming *b*, and a third *c*, which is bursting and throwing out the spores. The *Aspergillus* and the *Penicillium* differ from the *Mucor* in having their spores naked and not enclosed in a sporecase. In *Penicillium* they grow like the beads of a necklace one above the other on the top of the upright tube, and can very easily be separated (see Fig. 22); while *Aspergillus*, a most lovely silvery mould, is more complicated in the growth of its spores, for it bears them on many rows branching out from the top of the tube like the rays of a star.

" I want you to look at each of these moulds carefully under the microscope, for few people who hastily scrape a mould away, vexed to find it on food or damp clothing, have any idea what a delicate and

Fig. 23.

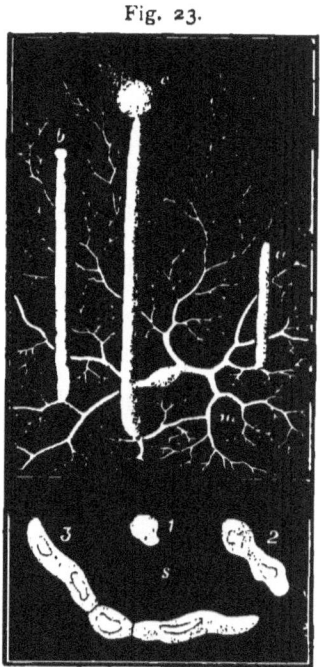

Mucor Mucedo, greatly magnified. (After Sachs and Brefeld.)

m, Mycelium, or tangle of threads. *a*, *b*, *c*, Upright tubes in different stages. *c*, Sporecase bursting and sending out spores. *s*, 1, 2, 3, A growing spore, in different stages, starting a new mycelium.

beautiful structure lies under their hand. These moulds live on decaying matter, but many of the mildews, rusts, and other kinds of fungus, prey upon living plants such as the *smut* of oats (*Ustilago carbo*), and the *bunt* (*Tilletia caria*) which eats away the inside of the grains of wheat, while another fungus attacks its leaves. There is scarcely a tree or herb which has not one fungus to prey upon it, and many have several, as, for example, the common lime-tree, which is infested by seventy-four different fungi, and the oak by no less than 200.

" So these colourless food-taking plants prey upon their neighbours, while they take their oxygen for breathing from air. The ' ferments,' however, which live *inside* plants or fluids, take even their oxygen for breathing from their hosts.

" If you go into the garden in summer and pluck an overripe gooseberry, which is bursting like this one I have here, you will probably find that the pulp looks unhealthy and rotten near the split, and the gooseberry will taste tart and disagreeable. This is because a small fungus has grown inside, and worked a change in the juice of the fruit. At first this fungus spread its tubes outside and merely *fed* upon the fruit, using oxygen from the air in breathing ; but by and by the skin gave way, and the fungus crept inside the gooseberry where it could no longer get any fresh air. In this dilemma it was forced to break up the sugar in the fruit and take the oxygen out of it, leaving behind only alcohol and carbonic acid which give the fermented taste to the fruit.

" So the fungus-imp feeds and grows in nature,

and when man gets hold of it he forces it to do the same work for a useful purpose, for the grape-fungus grows in the vats in which grapes are crushed and kept away from air, and tearing up the sugar, leaves alcohol behind in the grape-juice, which in this way becomes wine. So, too, the yeast-fungus grows in the malt and hop liquor, turning it into beer ; its spores floating in the fluid and increasing at a marvellous rate, as any housewife knows who, getting yeast for her bread, tries to keep it in a corked bottle.

"The yeast plant has never been found wild. It is only known as a cultivated plant, growing on prepared liquor. The brewer has to sow it by taking some yeast from other beer, or by leaving the liquor exposed to air in which yeast spores are floating ; or it will sow itself in the same way in a mixture of water, hops, sugar, and salt, to which a handful of flour is added. It increases at a marvellous rate, one cell budding out of another, while from time to time the living matter in a cell will break up into four parts instead of two, and so four new cells will start and bud. A drop of yeast will very soon cover a glass slide with this tiny plant, as you will see under the second microscope, where they are now at work (Fig. 24).

Fig. 24.

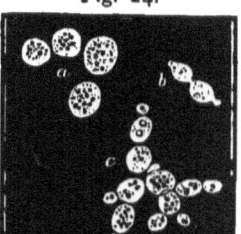

Yeast cells growing under the microscope. *a*, Single cells. *b*, Two cells forming by division. *c*, A group of cells where division is going on in all directions.

"But perhaps the most curious of all the minute fungi are those which grow inside insects and destroy them. At this time of year you may often see a dead fly sticking to the window-pane with a cloudy white ring round it ; this poor fly has been killed by a little fungus called *Empusa muscæ*. A spore from a former plant has fallen perhaps on the window-pane, or some other spot over which the fly has crawled, and being sticky has fixed itself under the fly's body. Once settled on a favourable spot it sends out a tube, and piercing the skin of the fly, begins to grow rapidly inside. There it forms little round cells one after the other, something like the yeast-cells, till it fills the whole body, feeding on its juices : then each cell sends a tube, like the upright tubes of the *Mucor* Fig. 23) out again through the fly's skin, and this tube bursts at the end, and so new spores are set free. It is these tubes, and the spores thrown from them, which you see forming a kind of halo round the dead fly as it clings to the pane. Other fungi in the same way kill the silk-worm and the caterpillars of the cabbage butterfly. Nor is it only the lower animals which suffer. When we once realise that fungus spores are floating every-where in the air, we can understand how the terrible microscopic fungi called *bacteria* will settle on an open wound and cause it to fester if it is not properly dressed.

"Thus we see that these minute fungi are almost everywhere. The larger ones, on the contrary, are confined to the fields and forests, damp walls and hollow trees ; or wherever rotting wood, leaves, or manure provide them with sufficient nourishment. Few people have any clear ideas about the growth

of a mushroom, except that the part we pick springs
up in a single night. The real fact is, that a whole
mushroom plant is nothing more than a gigantic
mould or mildew, only that it is formed of many
different shaped
cells, and spreads
its tubes *under-
ground* or through
the trunks of trees
instead of in paste
or jam, as in the
case of the mould.

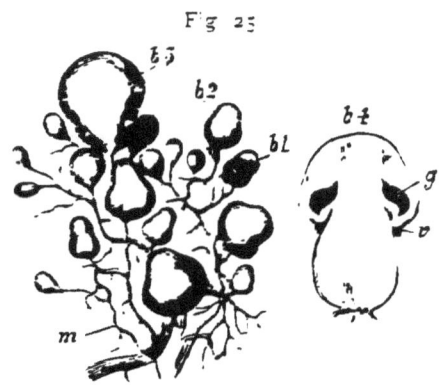

Fig 25

"The part which
we gather and call a
mushroom, a toad-
stool, or a puffball is
only the fruit, answer-
ing to the round balls
of the mould. The
rest of the plant is
a thick network of

Early stages of the mushroom.
After Sachs.

m Mycelium. *b1-3.* Mushroom buds of
different ages. *4* Button mushroom. *5*
Gills forming inside before lower attach-
ment of the cap gives way at *c*.

tubes, which you will see under the third microscope. These tubes spread underground and suck
in decayed matter from the earth; they form the
mycelium '*m*, Fig. 25, such as we found in the
mould. The mushroom-growers call it 'mushroom
spawn' because they use it to spread over the
ground for new crops. Out of these underground
tubes there springs up from time to time a
swollen round body no bigger at first than a mustard
seed *b1*. Fig. 25 . As it increases in size it comes
above ground and grows into the mushroom or

spore-case, answering to the round balls which
contain the spores of the mould.   At first this
swollen body is egg-shaped, the top half being
largest and broadest, and the fruit is then called
a 'button-mushroom' *b*4.   Inside this ball are
now formed a series of folds made of long cells,
some of which are soon to bear spores just as the

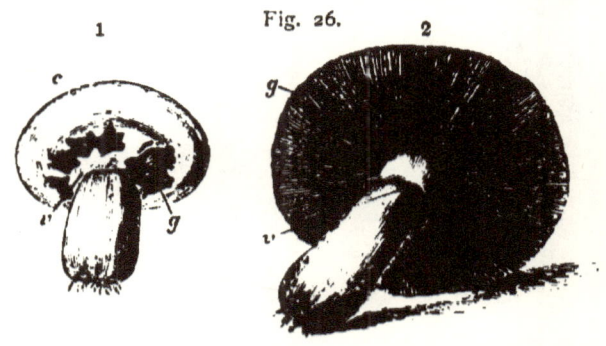

Fig. 26.

Later stages of the mushroom.   (After Gautier.)

1, Button mushroom stage.   *c*, Cap.   *v*, Veil.   *g*, Gills.

2, Full-grown mushroom, showing veil *v* after the cap is quite
free, and the gills or lamellæ *g*, of which the structure is shown in
Fig. 27.

tubes in the mould did, and while these are forming
and ripening, a way out is preparing for them.   For
as the mushroom grows, the skin of the lower part
of the ball (*v*, *b*4) is stretched more and more, till it
can bear the strain no longer and breaks away from
the stalk ; then the ball expands into an umbrella,
leaving a piece of torn skin, called the veil (*v*, Fig. 26),
clinging to the stalk.

     "All this happens in a single night, and the mush-
room is complete, with a stem up the centre and a

broad cap, under which are the folds which bear the
spores. Thus much you can see for yourselves at any
time by finding a place where mushrooms grow and
looking for them late at night and early in the
morning so as to get the different stages. But now

Fig. 27.

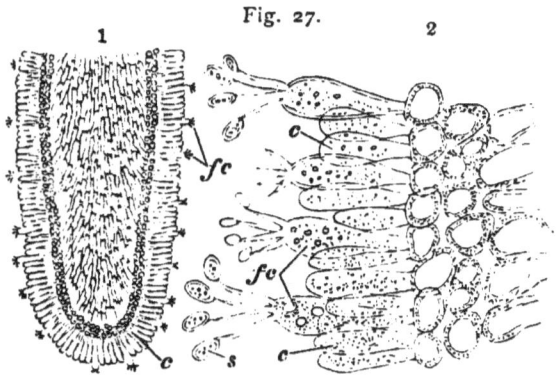

1, One of the gills or lamellæ of the mushroom slightly magnified,
showing the cells round the edge. *c*, Cells which do not bear
spores. *fc*, Fertile cells. 2, A piece of the edge of the same
powerfully magnified, showing how the spores *s* grow out of the
tip of the fertile cells *fc*.

we must turn to the microscope, and cutting off one
of the folds, which branch out under the cap like the
spokes of a wheel, take a slice across it (1, Fig. 27)
and examine.

"First, under a moderate power, you will see the
cells forming the centre of the fold and the layer of
long cells (*c* and *fc*) which are closely packed all round
the edge. Some of these cells project beyond the
others, and it is they which bear the spores. We
see this plainly under a very strong power when you
can distinguish the sterile cells *c* and the fertile cells

fc projecting beyond them, and each bearing four spore-cells *s* on four little horns at its tip.

"These spores fall off very easily, and you can make a pretty experiment by cutting off a large mushroom head in the early morning and putting it flat upon a piece of paper. In a few hours, if you lift it very carefully, you will find a number of dark lines on the paper, radiating from a centre like the spokes of a wheel, each line being composed of the spores which have fallen from a fold as it grew ripe. They are so minute that many thousands would be required to make up the size of the head of an ordinary pin, yet if you gather the spores of the several kinds of mushroom, and examine them under a strong microscope, you will find that even these specks of matter assume different shapes in the various species.

"You will be astonished too at the immense number of spores contained in a single mushroom head, for they are reckoned by millions; and when we remember that each one of these is the starting point of a new plant, it reminds us forcibly of the wholesale destruction of spores and seeds which must go on in nature, otherwise the mushrooms and their companions would soon cover every inch of the whole world.

"As it is, they are spread abroad by the wind, and wherever they escape destruction they lie waiting in every nook and corner till, after the hot summer, showers of rain hasten the decay of plants and leaves, and then the mushrooms, toadstools, and puffballs, grow at an astounding pace. If you go into the woods at this season you may see the enormous deep-red liver fungus (*Fistulina hepatica*) growing on the oak-trees, in patches which weigh from twenty to thirty pounds ; or the glorious orange-coloured fungus (*Tremella mesenterica*) growing on bare sticks or stumps of furze ; or among dead leaves you may easily chance on the little caps of the crimson, scarlet, snowy white, or orange-coloured fungi which grow in almost every wood. From white to yellow, yellow to red, red to crimson and purple black, there is hardly any colour you may not find among this gaily-decked tribe ; and who can wonder that the small bright-coloured caps have been supposed to cover tiny imps or elves, who used the large mushrooms to serve for their stools and tables ?

" There they work, thrusting their tubes into twigs and dead branches, rotting trunks and decaying leaves, breaking up the hard wood and tough fibres, and building them up into delicate cells, which by and by die and leave their remains as food for the early growing plants in the spring. So we see that in their way the mushrooms and toadstools are good imps after all, for the tender shoot of a young seedling plant could take no food out of a hard tree-trunk, but it finds the work done for it by the fungus, the rich nourishment being spread around its young roots ready to be imbibed.

" To find our fairy-ring mushrooms, however, we must leave the wood and go out into the open country, especially on the downs and moors and rough meadows, where the land is poor and the grass coarse and spare. There grow the nourishing kinds, most of which we can eat, and among these is the

8

delicate little champignon or 'Scotch-bonnet' mushroom, *Marasmius Oreades*,[1] which makes the fairy-
rings. When a spore of this mushroom begins to
grow, it sucks up vegetable food out of the earth and
spreads its tubes underground, in all directions from
the centre, so that the mycelium forms a round patch
like a thick underground circular cobweb. In the
summer and autumn, when the weather is suitable, it
sends up its delicate pale-brown caps, which we may
gather and eat without stopping the growth of the
plant.

"This goes on year after year underground, new
tubes always travelling outwards till the circle widens
and widens like the rings of water on a pond, only
that it spreads very slowly, making a new ring each
year, which is often composed of a mass of tubes as
much as a foot thick in the ground, and the tender
tubes in the centre die away as the new ones form a
larger hoop outside.

"But all this is below ground; where then are
our fairy rings? Here is the secret. The tubes, as
we have seen, take up food from the earth and
build it up into delicate cells, which decay very soon,
and as they die make a rich manure at the roots of
the grass. So each season the cells of last year's ring
make a rich feeding-ground for the young grass,
which springs up fresh and green in a fairy ring,
while *outside* this emerald circle the mushroom tubes
are still growing and increasing underneath the grass,
so that next year, when the present ring is no longer
richly fed, and has become faded and brown like the

---

[1] Shown in initial letter of this chapter.

rest of the moor, another ring will spring up outside
it, feeding on the prepared food below.

" In bad seasons, though the tubes go on spreading
and growing below, the mushroom fruit does not
always appear above ground. The plant will only
fruit freely when the ground has been well warmed
by the summer sun, followed by damp weather to
moisten it. This gives us a rich crop of mushrooms
all over the country, and it is then you can best
see the ring of fairy mushrooms circling outside the
green hoop of fresh grass. In any case the early
morning is the time to find them ; it is only in very
sheltered spots that they sometimes last through the
day, or come up towards evening, as I found them
last night on the warm damp side of the dell.

" This is the true history of fairy rings, and now go
and look for yourselves under the microscopes.
Under the first three you will find the three different
kinds of mould of our diagram (Fig. 22). Under the
fourth the spores of the mould are shown in their
first growth putting out the tubes to form the
mycelium. The fifth shows the mould itself with its
fruit-bearing tubes, one of which is bursting. Under
the sixth the yeast plant is growing ; the seventh
shows a slice of one of the folds of the common
mushroom with its spore-bearing horns ; and under
the eighth I have put some spores from different
mushrooms, that you may see what curious shapes
they assume.

" Lastly, let me remind you, now that the autumn
and winter are coming, that you will find mushrooms, toadstools, puffballs, and moulds in plenty

wherever you go.   Learn to know them, their different shapes and colours, and above all the special
nooks each one chooses for its home.   Look around
in the fields and woods and take note of the decaying plants and trees, leaves and bark, insects and
dead remains of all kinds.   Upon each of these you
will find some fungus growing, breaking up their
tissues and devouring the nourishing food they provide.   Watch these spots, and note the soft spongy
soil which will collect there, and then when the
spring comes, notice what tender plants flourish upon
these rich feeding grounds.   You will thus see for
yourselves that the fungi, though they feed upon
others, are not entirely mischief-workers, but also
perform their part in the general work of life."

CHAPTER IV

THE LIFE-HISTORY OF LICHENS AND MOSSES

THE autumn has passed away and we are in the midst of winter. In the long winter evenings the stars shine bright and clear, and tempt us to work with the telescope and its helpmates the spectroscope and photographic plates. But at first sight it would seem as though our microscopes would have to stand idle so far at least as plants are concerned, or be used only to examine dried specimens and mounted sections. Yet this is not the fact, as I remembered last week when walking through the bare and leafless wood. A startled pheasant rising with a whirr at the sound of my footsteps among the dead leaves roused me from my thoughts, and as a young rabbit scudded across the path and I watched it disappear among the bushes, I was suddenly struck with the great mass of plant life flourishing underfoot and overhead.

Can you guess what plants these were? I do not mean the evergreen pines and firs, nor the few hardy ferns, nor the lovely ivy clothing the trunks of the trees. Such plants as these live and remain green in the winter, but they do not grow. If you wish to find plant life revelling in the cold damp days of winter, fearing neither frost nor snow and welcoming mist and rain, you must go to the mosses, which as autumn passes away begin to cover the wood-paths, to creep over the roots of the trees, to suck up the water in the bogs, and even to clothe dead walls and stones with a soft green carpet. And with the mosses come the lichens, those curious grey and greenish oddities which no one but a botanist would think of classing among plants.

The wood is full of them now : the hairy lichens hang from the branches of many of the trees, making them look like old greybearded men ; the leafy lichens encircle the branches, their pale gray, green, and yellow patches looking as if they were made of crumpled paper cut into wavy plates ; and the crusty lichens, scarcely distinguishable from the bark of the trees, cover every available space which the mosses have left free.

As I looked at these lichens and thought of their curious history I determined that we would study them to-day, and gathered a basketful of specimens (see Fig. 28). But when I had collected these I found I had not the heart to leave the mosses behind. I could not even break off a piece of bark with lichen upon it without some little moss coming too, especially the small thread-mosses *(Bryum)* which make a

Fig. 28.

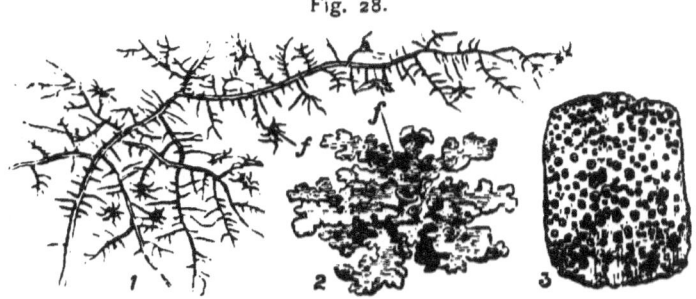

Examples of Lichens. (From life.)
1, A hairy lichen. 2, A leafy lichen. 3, A crustaceous lichen.
f. f, the fruit.

home for themselves in every nook and corner of the branches ; while the feather-mosses, hair-mosses, cord-mosses, and many others made such a lovely carpet under my feet that each seemed too beautiful to pass by, and they found their way into my basket, crowned at the top with a large mass of the pale-green Sphagnum, or bog-moss, into which I sank more than ankle-deep as I crossed the bog in the centre of the wood on my way home.

So here they all are, and I hope by the help of our magic glass to let you into some of the secrets of their lives. It is true we must study the structure of lichens chiefly by diagrams, for it is too minute for beginners to follow under the microscope, so we must trust to drawings made by men more skilful in microscopic botany, at any rate for the present. But the mosses we can examine for ourselves and admire their delicate leaves and wonderful tiny spore-cases.

Now the first question which I hope you want to ask is, how it is that these lowly plants flourish so well in the depth of winter when their larger and stronger companions die down to the ground. We will answer this first as to the lichens, which are such strange uncanny-looking plants that it is almost difficult to imagine they are alive at all ; and indeed they have been a great puzzle to botanists.

Before we examine them, however, look for a minute at a small drop of this greenish film which I have taken from the rain-water taken outside. I have put some under each microscope, and those who can look into them will see the slide almost covered with small round green cells very much like the yeast cells we saw when studying the Fungi, only that instead of being colourless they are a bright green. Some of these cells will I suspect be longer than others, and these long cells will be moving over the slide very rapidly, swimming hither and thither, and you will see, perhaps for the first time, that very low plants can swim about in water. These green cells are, indeed, the simplest of all plants, and are merely bags of living matter which, by the help of the green granules in them, are able to work up water and gases into nourishing food, and so to live, grow, and multiply.

Fig. 29.

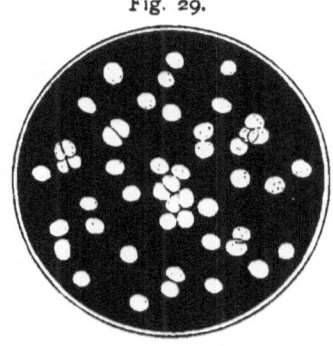

Single-celled green plants growing and dividing (*Pleurococcus*). (After Thuret and Bornet.)

There are many kinds of these single-celled plants in the world. You may find them on damp paths, in almost any rain-water butt, in ponds and ditches, in sparkling waterfalls, along the banks of flowing rivers, and in the cold clear springs on the bleak mountains. Some of them take the form of tangled threads [1] composed of long strings of cells, and these sometimes form long streamers in flowing water, and at other times are gathered together in a shapeless film only to be disentangled under a microscope. Other kinds [2] wave to and fro on the water, forming dense patches of violet, orange-brown, or glossy green scum shining in the bright sunlight, and these flourish equally in the ponds of our gardens and in pools in the Himalaya mountains, 18,000 feet above the sea. Others again [3] seize on every damp patch on tree trunks, rocks, or moist walls, covering them with a green powder formed of single plant cells. Other species of this family turn a bright red colour when the cells are still ; and one, under the name of Gory Dew, [4] has often frightened the peasants of Italy, by growing very rapidly over damp walls and then turning the colour of blood. Another [5] forms the "red snow" of the Arctic regions, where it covers wide surfaces of snow with a deep red colour. Others [6] form a shiny jelly over rocks and stones, and these may be found almost everywhere, from the garden path to the warm springs of India, from the marshes of New Zealand up to the shores of the Arctic ocean, and even on the surface of floating icebergs.

[1] *Confervæ.*   [2] *Oscillariæ.*   [3] *Protococcus.*
[4] *Palmella cruenta.*   [5] *Protococcus nivalis.*   [6] *Nostoc.*

The reason why these plants can live in such very different regions is that they do not take their food through roots out of the ground, but suck in water and gases through the thin membrane which covers their cell, and each cell does its own work. So it matters very little to them where they lie, so long as they have moisture and sunlight to help them in their work. Wherever they are, if they have these, they can take in carbonic acid from the air and work up the carbon with other gases which they imbibe with the water, and so make living material. In this way they grow, and as a cell grows larger the covering is stretched and part of the digested food goes to build up more covering membrane, and by and by the cell divides into two and each membrane closes up, so that there are two single-celled plants where there was only one before. This will sometimes go on so fast that a small pond may be covered in a few hours with a green film formed of new cells.

Now we have seen, when studying mushrooms, that the one difference between these green plants and the single-celled Fungi is that while the green cells make their own food, colourless cells can only take it in ready-made, and therefore prey upon all kinds of living matter. This is just what happens in the lichens ; and botanists have discovered that these curious growths are really the result of a *partnership* between single-celled green plants and single-celled fungi. The grey part is a fungus ; but when it is examined under the microscope we find it is not a fungus only ; a number of green cells can be seen scattered through it, which, when carefully studied, prove to be some species of the green single-celled plants.

Here are two drawings of sections cut through two different lichens, and enormously magnified so that the cells are clearly seen. 1, Fig. 30 is part of a hairy lichen (1, Fig. 28), and 2 is part of a leafy lichen (2, Fig. 28). The hairy lichen as you see has a row of green cells all round the tiny branch, with fungus cells on all sides of them. The leafy lichen, which only presents one surface to the sun and air while the other side is against the tree, has only one layer of green cells near the surface, but protected by the fungus above.

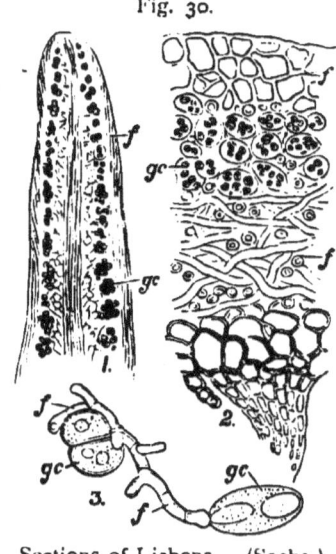

Fig. 30.

Sections of Lichens. (Sachs.) 1, Section of a hairy lichen, *Usnea barbata.* 2, Section of a leafy lichen, *Sticta fuliginosa.* 3, Early growth of a lichen. *gc*, Green cells. *f*, Fungus.

The way the lichen has grown is this. A green cell (*gc* 3, Fig. 30) falling on some damp spot has begun to grow and spread, working up food in the sunlight. To it comes the spore of the fungus *f*, first thrusting its tubes into the tree-bark, or wall, and then spreading round the green cells, which remain always in such a position that sunlight, air, and moisture can reach them. From this time the two classes of plants live as friends, the fungus using part of the food made by the green cells, and giving them in return the advantage of being spread out to the sunlight, while they are also protected in frosty or sultry weather when they would dry up on a bare surface.   On the whole, however, the fungus probably gains the most, for it has been found, as we should expect, that the green cells can live and grow if separated out of the lichen, but the fungus cells die when their industrious companions are taken from them.

At any rate the partnership succeeds, as you will see if you go into the wood, or into an orchard where the apple-trees are neglected, for every inch of the branches is covered by lichens if not already taken up by mosses or toadstools.

There is hardly any part of the world except the tropics where lichens do not abound.   In the Alps of Scandinavia close to the limits of perpetual snow, in the sandy wastes of Arctic America, and over the dreary Tundras of Arctic Siberia, where the ground is frozen hard during the greater part of the year, they flourish where nothing else can live.

The little green cells multiply by dividing, as we saw them doing in the green film from the water-butt.   The fungus, however, has many different modes of seeding itself.   One of these is by form-ing little pockets in the lichen, out of which, when they burst, small round bodies are thrown, which cover the lichen with a minute green powder.   There is plenty of this powder on the leafy lichen which you have by you.   You can see it with the magnifying-glass, without putting it under the microscope. As long as the lichen is dry these round bodies do not grow, but as soon as moisture reaches them they start away and become new plants.

A more complicated and beautiful process is shown in this diagram (Fig. 31). If you look carefully at the leafy lichen (2, Fig. 28) you will find here and there some little cups *f*, while others grow upon the

Fig. 31.

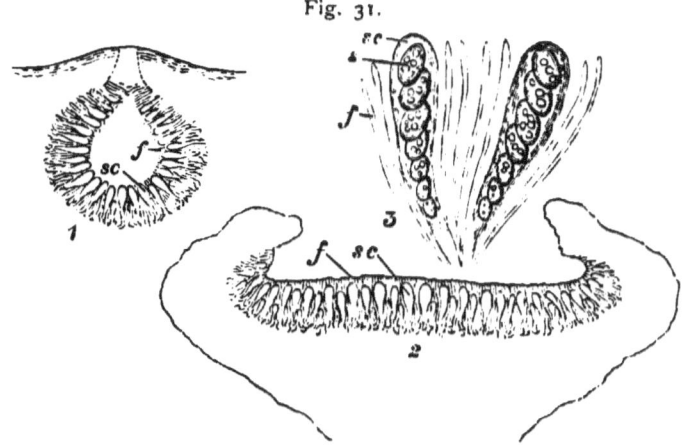

Fructification of a lichen. (From Sachs and Oliver.)
Apothecium or spore-chamber of a lichen. 1, Closed. 2, Open. 3, The spore-cases and filaments enlarged, showing the spores. *f*, Filaments. *sc*, Spore-cases. *s*, Spores.

tips of the hairy lichen. These cups, or fruits, were once closed, flask-shaped chambers (1, Fig. 31) inside which are formed a number of oval cells *sc*, which are spore-cases, with from four to eight spores or seed-like bodies *s*3 inside them. When these chambers, which are called *apothecia*, are ripe, moist or rainy weather causes them to swell at the top, and they burst open and the spore-cases throw out the spores to grow into new fungi.

In some lichens the chambers remain closed and the spores escape through a hole in the top, and they are then called *perithecia*, while in others, as these which we have here, they open out into a cup-shape.

This, then, is the curious history of lichens ; the green cells and fungi flourishing together in the damp winter and bearing the hardest frost far better than the summer drought, so that they have their good time when most other plants are dead or asleep. Yet though some of them, such as the hairy lichens, almost disappear in the summer, they are by no means dead, for, like all these very low plants, they can bear being dried up for a long time, and then, when moisture visits them again, each green cell sets to work, and they revive. There is much more to be learnt about them, but this will be sufficient to make you feel an interest in their simple lives, and when you look for them in the wood you will be surprised to find how many different kinds there are, for it is most wonderful that such lowly plants should build up such an immense variety of curious and grotesque forms.

.　　　.　　　.　　　.　　　.

And yet, when we turn to the mosses, I am half afraid they will soon attract you away from the dull grey lichens, for of all plant histories it appears to me that the history of the moss-plant is most fascinating.

As this history is complicated by the moss having, as it were, two lives, you must give me your whole attention, and I will explain it first from diagrams, though you can see all the steps under the microscope.

Take in your hands, in the first place, a piece of this green moss which I have brought. How thick it is, like a rich felted carpet! and yet, if you pull it apart carefully, you will find that each leafy stem is separate, and can be taken away from the others without breaking anything. In this dense moss each stem is single and clothed with leaves wrapped closely round it (see Fig. 33); in some mosses the stem is branched, and in others the leaves grow on side stalks, as in this feathery moss (Fig. 32). But in each case every stem is like a separate plant, with its own tuft of tender roots *r*.

Fig. 32.

A stem of feathery moss. (From life.) *l*, Leaves. *s*, Stem. *r*, Roots.

What a delicate growth it is! The stem is scarcely more than a fine thread, the leaves minute, transparent, and tender. In this pale sphagnum or bog-moss (Fig. 36, p. 93), which is much larger and stouter, you can see better how each one of these leaves, though they are so thickly packed, is placed so that it can get the utmost light, air, and moisture. Yet so closely are the leaves of each stem entangled in those of the next that the whole forms a thick springy green carpet under our feet.

How is it, then, that these moss stems, though each independent, grow in such a dense mass? Partly because moss multiplies so rapidly that new

stems are always thrusting themselves up to the
light, but chiefly because the stems were not always
separate, but in very early life sprang from a
common source.

If, instead of bringing the moss home and tearing
it apart, you went to a spot in the wood where fresh
moss was growing, and looked very carefully on
the surface of the ground or among the water
of a marsh, you would find a spongy green mass
below the growing moss, very much like the green
scum on a pond. This film, some of which I
have brought home, is seen under the microscope
to be a mass of tangled green threads (*t*, Fig. 34,
p. 88) like those of the *Conferva* (see p. 79), composed of rows of cells, while here and there upon
these threads you would find a bud (*mb*, Fig. 34)
rising up into the air.

This tangled mass of green threads, called the
protonema, is the first growth, from which the moss
stems spring. It has itself originated from a moss-
spore; as we shall see by and by. As soon as it has
started it grows and spreads very rapidly, drinking
in water and air through all its cells and sending up
the moss buds which swell and grow, giving out roots
below and fine stems above, which soon become
crowded with leaves, forming the velvety carpet we
call moss. Meanwhile the soft threads below die
away, giving up all their nourishment to the moss-
stems, and this is why, when you take up the moss,
you find each stem separate. But now comes the
question, How does each stem live after the nourishing
threads below have died? It is true each stem has

a few hairy roots, but these are very feeble, and not at all like the roots of higher plants. The fact is, the moss is built up entirely of tender cells, like the green cells in the lichen, or in the film upon the pond. These cells are not shut in behind a thick skin as in the leaves of higher plants, but have every one of them the power to take in water and gases through their tender membrane.

Fig. 33.

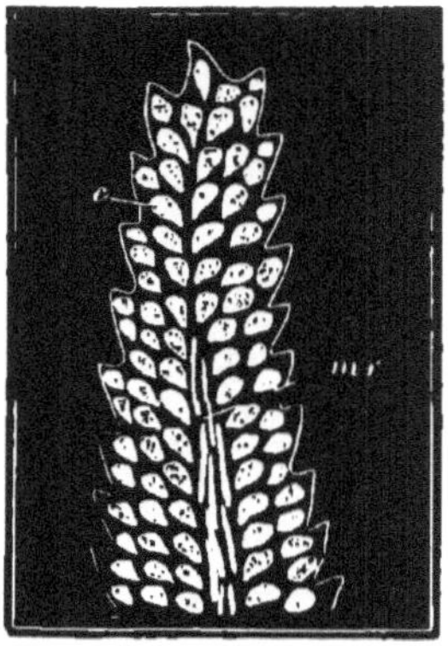

Moss-leaf magnified.
(From life.)
Showing the cells *c*, each of which can take in and work up its own food. *mr*, Long cells of the midrib.

I made last night a rough drawing of the leaf of the feathery moss put under the microscope, but you will see it far better by putting a leaf with a little water on a glass slide under the covering glass and examining it for yourself. You will see that it is composed of a number of oval-shaped cells packed closely together (*c* Fig. 33), with a few long narrow ones *mr* in the middle of the leaf forming the midrib. Every cell is as clear and distinct as if it were floating in the water, and the tiny green grains which help it to work up its food are clearly visible.

Each of these cells can act as a separate plant, drinking in the water and air it needs, and feeding and growing quite independently of the roots below. Yet at the same time the moss stem has a great advantage over single-celled plants in having root-hairs, and being able to grow upright and expose its leaves to the sun and air.

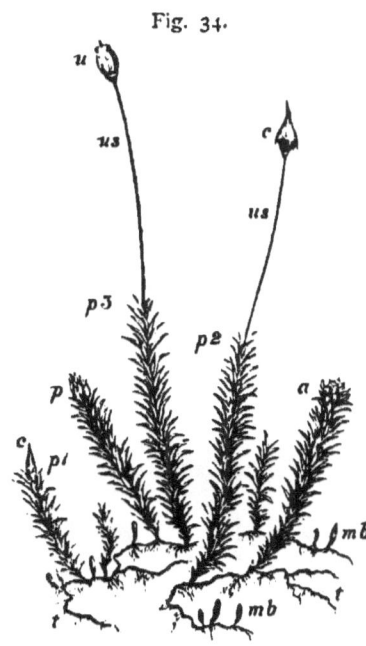

Fig. 34.

Polytrichum commune. A large hair-moss.

t, t, Threads of green cells forming the *protonema* out of which moss-buds spring. *mb,* Buds of moss-stems. *a,* Minute green flower in which the antherozoids are formed (enlarged in Fig. 35). *p, p1, p2, p3,* Minute green flower in which the ovules are formed, and urn-plant springing out of it (enlarged in Fig. 35). *us,* Urn stems. *c,* Cap. *u,* Urn after cap has fallen off, still protected by its lid.

Now you will no longer wonder that moss grows so fast and so thick, and another curious fact follows from the independence of each cell, namely, that new growths can start from almost any part of the plant. For example, pieces will often break off from the tangled mass or protonema below, and, starting on their own account, form other thread masses. Then, after the moss stems have grown, a new mass of threads may grow from one of the tiny root-hairs of a stem and make a fresh tangle; nay, a thread will sometimes even spring out of a damp moss leaf and make a new beginning, while the moss stems themselves often put forth buds and branches, which grow root-hairs and settle down on their own account.

All this comes from the simple nature of the plants, each cell doing its own work. Nor are the mosses in any difficulty as to soil, for as the matted threads decay they form a rich manure, and the dying moss-stems themselves, being so fragile, turn back very readily into food. This is why mosses can spread over the poorest soil where even tough grasses cannot live, and clothe walls and roofs with a rich green.

So far, then, we now understand the growth of the mossy-leaf stems, but this is only half the life of the plant. After the moss has gone on through the damp winter spreading and growing, there appear in the spring or summer tiny moss flowers at the tip of

Fig. 35.

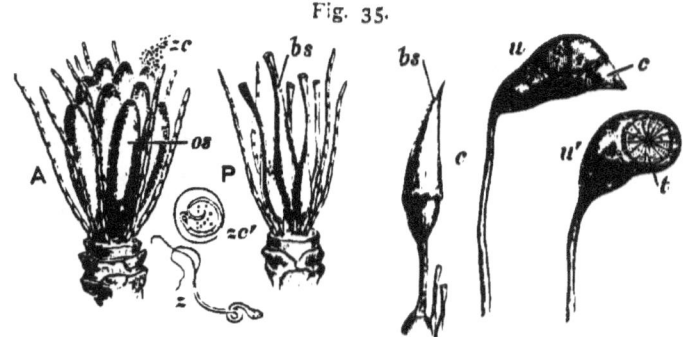

Fructification of a moss.

A, Male moss-flower stripped of its outer leaves, showing jointed filaments and oval sacs *os* and antherozoid cells *zc* swarming out of a sac. *zc'*, Antherozoid cell enlarged. *z*, Free antherozoid. P, Female flower with bottle-shaped sacs *bs*. *bs-c*, Bottle-shaped sac, with cap being pushed up. *u*, Urn of *Funaria hygrometrica*, with small cap. *u'*, Urn, from which the cap has fallen, showing the teeth *t* which keep in the spores.

some of the stems. These flowers (*a, p,* Fig. 34) are formed merely of a few green leaves shorter and stouter than the rest, enclosing some oval sacs surrounded by jointed hairs or filaments (see A and P, Fig. 35). These sacs are of two different kinds, one set being short and stout *os*, the others having long necks like bottles *bs*. Sometimes these two kinds of sac are in one flower, but more often they are in separate flowers, as in the hair-moss, *Polytrichum commune* (*a* and *p*, Fig. 34). Now when the flowers are ripe the short sacs in the flower A open and fling out myriads of cells *sc*, and these cells burst, and forth come tiny wriggling bodies *z*, called by botanists *antherozoids*, one out of each cell. These find their way along the damp moss to the flower P, and entering the neck of one of the bottle-shaped sacs *bs*, find out each another cell or *ovule* inside. The two cells together then form a *plant-egg*, which answers to the germ in the seeds of higher plants.

Now let us be sure we understand where we are in the life of the plant. We have had its green-growing time, its flowering, and the formation of what we may roughly call its seed, which last in ordinary higher plants would fall down and grow into a new green plant. But with the moss there is more to come. The egg does not shake out of the bottle-necked sac, but begins to grow inside it, sending down a little tube into the moss stem, and using it as other plants use the ground to grow in.

As soon as it is rooted it begins to form a delicate stem, and as this grows it pushes up the sac *bs*, stretching the neck tighter and tighter till at last it tears away below, and the sac is carried up and hangs like an extinguisher or cap (*c* Figs. 34, 35) over the top of the stem. Meanwhile, under this cap the top

of the stalk swells into a knob which, by degrees, becomes a lovely little covered urn *u*, something like a
poppy head, which has within it a number of spores.
The growth of this tiny urn-plant often occupies several
months, for you must remember that it is not merely
a fruit, though it is often called so, but a real plant,
taking in food through its tubes below and working
for its living.

When it is finished it is a most lovely little object
(*us*, Fig. 34), the fine hairlike stalk being covered with
a green, yellow, or brilliant red fool's cap on the top,
yet the whole in most mosses is not bigger than an
ordinary pin. You may easily see them in the spring
or summer, or even sometimes in the winter. I have
only been able to bring you one very little one to-
day, the *Funaria hygrometrica*, which fruits early in
the year. This moss has only a short cap, but
in many mosses they are very conspicuous. I have
often pulled them off as you would pull a cap from
a boy's head. In nature they fall off after a time,
leaving the urn, which, though so small, is a most
complicated structure. First it has an outer skin,
with holes or mouths in it which open and close to
let moisture in and out. Then come two layers of
cells, then an open space full of air, in which are
the green chlorophyll grains which are working
up food for the tiny plant as the moisture comes
in to them. Lastly, within this again is a mass
of tissue, round which grow the spores which are
soon to be sown, and which in *Polytrichum commune* are protected by a lid. Even after the
extinguisher and the lid have both fallen off, the

spores cannot fall out, for a thick row of teeth (*t*, Fig. 35) is closed over them like the tentacles of an anemone. So long as the air is damp these teeth remain closed ; it is only in fine dry weather that they open and the spores are scattered on the ground. *Funaria hygrometrica* has no lid under its cap, and after the cap falls the spores are only protected by the teeth.

When the spores are gone, the life of the tiny urn-plant is over. It shrivels and dies, leaving ten, fifteen, or even more spores, which, after lying for some time on the ground, sprout and grow into a fresh mass of soft threads.

So now we have completed the life-history of the moss and come back to the point at which we started. I am afraid it has been rather a difficult history to follow step by step, and yet it is perfectly clear when once we master the succession of growths. Starting from a spore, the thread-mass or protonema gives rise to the moss-stems forming the dense green carpet, then the green flowers on some of the leaf-stems give rise to a plant-egg, which roots itself in the stem, and grows into a perfect plant without leaves, bearing merely the urn in which fresh spores are formed, and so the round goes on from year to year.

There are a great number of different varieties of moss, and they differ in the shape and arrangement of their stems and leaves, and very much in the formation of their urns, yet this sketch will enable you to study them with understanding, and when you find in the wood the nodding caps of the fruit-ing plants, some red, some green, some yellow, and some a brilliant orange, you will feel that they are acquaintances, and by the help of the microscope may soon become friends.

Among them one of the most interesting is the sphagnum or bog-moss (Fig. 36), which spreads its thick carpet over all the bogs in the woods. You cannot miss its little orange-coloured spore-cases if you look closely, for they contrast strongly with its pale green leaves, out of which they stand on very short stalks. I wish we could examine it, for it differs much from other mosses. both in leaves and fruit, but it would take us too long. At least, however, you must put one of its lovely transparent leaves under the microscope, that you may see the large air-cells which lie between the growing cells, and admire the lovely glistening bands which run across and across their covering membrane, for the sphagnum leaf is so extremely beautiful that you will never forget it when once seen. It is through these large cells in the edge of the stem and leaf that the water rises up from the swamp, so that the whole moss is like a wet sponge.

Fig. 36.

Sphagnum moss from a Devonshire bog. (From life.)

And now, before we part, we had better sum up the history of lichens and mosses. With the lichens we have seen that the secret of success seems to be mutual help. The green cells provide the food, the fungus cells form a surface over which the green cells can spread to find sunlight and moisture, and protection from extremes of heat or cold. With the mosses the secret lies in their standing on the borderland between two classes of plant life. On the one hand, they are still tender-celled plants, each cell being able to live its own life and make its own food; on the other hand, they have risen into shapely plants with the beginnings of feeble roots, and having stems along which their leaves are arranged so that they are spread to the light and air. Both lichens and mosses keep one great advantage common to all tender-celled plants; they can be dried up so that you would think them dead, and yet, because they can work all over their surface whenever heat and moisture reach them, each cell drinks in food again and the plant revives. So when a scorching sun, or a dry season, or a biting frost kills other plants, the mosses and lichens bide their time till moisture comes again.

In our own country they grow almost every-where—on walls, on broken ground, on sand-heaps, on roofs and walls, on trees living and dead, and over all pastures which are allowed to grow poor and worn out. They grow, too, in all damp, marshy spots; especially the bog-mosses forming the peat-bogs which cover a large part of Ireland and many regions in Scotland; and these same bog-mosses occur in America, New Zealand, and Australia.

In the tropics mosses are less abundant, probably

because other plants flourish so luxuriantly ; but in Arctic Siberia and Arctic America both lichens and mosses live on the vast Tundras. There, during the three short months of summer, when the surface of the ground is soft, the lichens spread far and wide where all else is lifeless, while in moister parts the Polytrichums or hair-mosses cover the ground, and in swampy regions stunted Sphagnums form peat-bogs only a few inches in depth over the frozen soil beneath. If, then, the lichens and mosses can flourish even in such dreary latitudes as these, we can understand how they defy even our coldest winters, appearing fresh and green when the snow melts away from over them, and leave their cells bathed in water, so that these lowly plants clothe the wood with their beauty when otherwise all would be bare and lifeless.

10

CHAPTER V

THE HISTORY OF A LAVA STREAM

T is now just twenty-two years ago, boys, since I saw a wonderful sight, which is still so fresh in my mind that I have to look round and remember that it was before any of you were born, in order to persuade myself that it can be nearly a quarter of a century since I stood with my feet close to a flowing stream of red-hot lava.

It happened in this way. I was spending the winter with friends in Naples, and we were walking quietly one lovely afternoon in November along the Villa Reale, the public garden on the sea-shore, when one of our party exclaimed, "Look at Vesuvius!" We did so, and saw in the bright sunlight a dense dark cloud rising up out of the cone. The mountain had been sending out puffs of smoke, with a booming noise, for several days, but we thought nothing of

that, for it had been common enough for slight
eruptions to take place at intervals ever since the
great eruption of 1867. This cloud, however, was far
larger and wider-spread than usual, and as we were
looking at it we saw a thin red line begin some way
down the side of the mountain and creep onwards

Fig. 37.

Somma.   Vesuvius.

Vesuvius, as seen in eruption by the author, November 1868.

toward the valley which lies behind the Hermitage
near where the Observatory is built (see Fig. 37).
"A crater has broken out on the slope," said our
host ; "it will be a grand sight to-night. Shall we go
up and see it ?" No sooner proposed than settled,
and one of the party started off at once to secure
horses and men before others engaged them.

It was about eight o'clock in the evening when we

started in a carriage for Resina, and alighting there, with buried Herculaneum under our feet, mounted our horses and set forward with the guides. Then followed a long ascent of about two hours and a half through the dark night. Silently and carefully we travelled on over the broad masses of slaggy lava of former years, along which a narrow horse-path had been worn ; and ever and anon we heard the distant booming in the crater at the summit, and caught sight of fresh gleams of light as we took some turning which brought the glowing peak into view.

Our object was to get as close as possible to the newly-opened crater in the mountain-side, and when we arrived on a small rugged plain not far from the spot, we alighted from our horses, which were growing frightened with the glare, and walked some distance on foot till we came to a ridge running down the slope, and upon this ridge the lava stream was flowing.

Above our heads hung a vast cloud of vapour which reflected the bright light from the red-hot stream, and threw a pink glow all around, so that, where the cloud was broken and we could see the dark sky, the stars looked white as silver in contrast. We could now trace clearly the outline of the summit towering above us, and even watch the showers of ashes and dust which burst forth from time to time, falling back into the crater, or on to the steep slopes of the cone.

If the night had not been calm, and such a breeze as there was blowing away from us, our position would scarcely have been safe ; and indeed we were afterwards told we had been rash. But I would have faced even a greater risk to see so grand a spectacle, and when the guide helped me to scramble up on to the ledge, so that I stood with my feet within a few yards of the lava flow, my heart bounded with excitement. I could not stay more than a few seconds, for the gases and vapour choked me ; but for that short time it felt like a dream to be standing close to a river of molten rock, which a few hours before had been lying deep in the bowels of the earth. Glancing upwards to where this river issued from the cone in the mountain-side, I saw it first white-hot, then gradually fading to a glowing red as it crept past my feet; and then looking down the slope I saw it turn black and gloomy as it cooled rapidly at the top, while through the cracks which opened here and there as it moved on, puffs of gas and vapour rose into the air, and the red lava beneath gleamed through the chinks.

We did not stay long, for the air was suffocating, but took our way back to the Hermitage, where another glorious sight awaited us. Some way above and behind the hill on which the Observatory stands there is, or was, a steep cliff, and over this the lava stream, now densely black, fell in its way to the valley below, and as it fell it broke into huge masses, which heeling over exposed the red-hot lava under the crust, thus forming a magnificent fiery cascade in which black and red were mingled in wild confusion.

This is how I saw a fresh red-hot lava stream. I had ascended the mountain some years before, when it was comparatively quiet, with only two

small cones in its central crater sending out miniature
flows of lava (see Fig. 38). But the crater was too
hot for me to cross over to these cones, and I could
only marvel at the mass of ashes of which the top of
the mountain was composed, and plunge a stick into
an old lava stream to see how hot it still remained

Fig. 38.

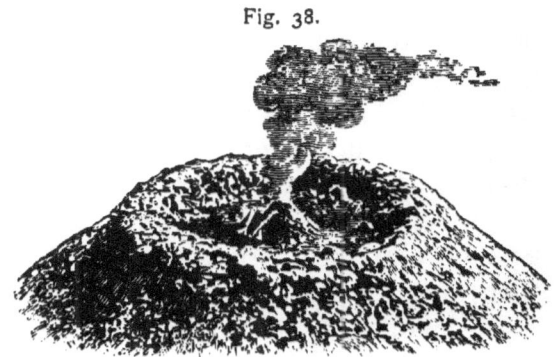

The top of Vesuvius in 1864. (After Nasmyth.)

below. Peaceful and quiet as the mountain seemed
then, I could never have imagined such a glorious
outburst as that of November 1868 unless I had
seen it, and yet this was quite a small eruption compared to those of 1867 and 1872, which in their
turn were nothing to some of the older eruptions in
earlier centuries.

Now it is the history of this lava stream which I
saw, that we are going to consider to-day, and you
will first want to know where it came from, and what
caused it to break out on the mountain-side. The
truth is, that though we know now a good deal about
volcanoes themselves, we know very little about the
mighty cauldrons deep down in the earth from which

they come. Our deepest mines only reach to a depth of a little more than half a mile, and no borings even have been made beyond three-quarters of a mile, so that after this depth we are left very much to guess-work.

We do know that the temperature increases as we go farther down from the surface, but the increase is very different in different districts—in some places being five times greater than it is in others at an equal depth, and it is always greatest in localities where volcanoes have been active not long before. Now if there were an ocean of melted rock at a certain distance down below the crust all over the globe, there could scarcely be such a great difference between one place and another, and for this and many other reasons geologists are inclined to think that, from some un-known cause, great heat is developed at special points below the surface at different times. This would account for our finding volcanic rocks in almost all parts of the world, even very far away from where there are any active volcanoes now.

But, as I have said, we do not clearly know why great reservoirs of melted rock occur from time to time deep under our feet. We may perhaps one day find the clue from the fact that nearly all, if not all, volcanoes occur near to the water's edge, either on the coast of the great oceans or of some enormous inland sea or lake. But at present all we can say is, that in certain parts of the globe there must be from time to time great masses of rock heated till they are white-hot, and having white-hot water mingled with them. These great masses need not, however, be liquid, for we know that under enormous pressure white-hot metals remain solid, and water instead of flashing into steam is kept liquid, pressing with tremendous force upon whatever keeps it confined.

But now suppose that for some reason the mass of solid rock and ground above one of these heated spots should crack and become weak, or that the pressure from below should become so great as to be more powerful than the weight above, then the white-hot rock and water quivering and panting to expand, would upheave and burst the walls of their prison. Cannot you picture to yourselves how when this happened the rock would swell into a liquid state, and how the water would force its way upwards into cracks and fissures expanding into steam as it went. Then would be heard strange rumbling noises underground, as all these heavily oppressed white-hot substances upheaved and rent the crust above them. And after a time the country round, or the ground at the bottom of the sea, would quake and tremble, till by and by a way out would be found, and the water flashing into vapour would break and fling up the masses of rock immediately above the passage it had made for itself, and following after these would come the molten rock pouring out at the new opening.

Such outbursts as these have been seen at sea many times near volcanic islands. In 1811 a new island called Sabrina was thrown up off St. Michael's in the Azores, and after remaining a short time was washed away by the waves. In the same way Graham's Island appeared off the coast of Sicily in

1831, and as late as 1885 Mr. Shipley saw a magnificent eruption in the Pacific near the Tonga Islands when an island about three miles long was formed.

Another very extraordinary outburst, this time on land, took place in 1538 on the opposite side of the Bay of Naples to where Vesuvius stands. There, on the shores of the Bay of Baiæ, a mountain 440 feet high was built up in one week, where all had before been quiet in the memory of man. For two years before the outburst came, rumblings and earthquakes had alarmed the people, and at last one day the sea drew back from the shore and the ground sank about fourteen feet, and then on the night of Sunday, September 29, 1538, it was hurled up again, and steam, fiery gases, stones, and mud burst forth, driving away the frightened people from the village of Puzzuoli about two miles distant. For a whole week jets of lava, fragments of rock, and showers of ashes were poured out, till they formed the hill now called Monte Nuovo, 440 feet high and measuring a mile and a half round the base. And there it has remained till the present day, perfectly quiet after the one great outburst had calmed down, and is now covered with thickets of stone-pine trees.

These sudden outbursts show that some great change must occur in the state of the earth's crust under the spots where they take place, and we know that eruptions may cease for centuries in any particular place and then begin afresh quite unexpectedly. Vesuvius was a peaceable mountain overgrown with trees and vines in the time of the Greeks till in the year A.D. 79 occurred the terrific outburst which destroyed Herculaneum and Pompeii, shattering old Vesuvius to pieces, so that only the cliffs on the north-west remain and are called Somma (see Fig. 37), while the new Vesuvius has grown up in the lap, as it were, of its old self. Yet when we visit the cliffs of Somma, and examine the old lava streams in them, we see that the ancient peaceful mountain was itself built up by volcanic outbursts of molten rock, and showers of clinkers or scoriæ, long before man lived to record it.

Meanwhile, when once an opening is made, we can understand how after an eruption is over, and the steam and lava are exhausted, all quiets down for awhile, and the melted rock in the crater of the mountain cools and hardens, shutting in once more the seething mass below. This was the state of the crater when I saw it in 1864, though small streams still flowed out of two minute cones ; but since then at least one great outburst had taken place in 1867, and now on this November night, 1868, the imprisoned gases rebelled once more and forced their way through the mountain-side.

At this point we can leave off forming conjectures and really study what happens ; for we do know a great deal about the structure of volcanoes themselves, and the history of a lava-flow has been made very clear during the last few years, chiefly by the help of the microscope and chemical experiments. If we imagine then that on the day of the eruption we could have seen the inside of the mountain, the diagram (Fig. 39) will fairly represent what was taking place there.

In the funnel *a* which passes down from the crater or cup *b*, *b*, white-hot lava was surging up, having a large quantity of water and steam entangled in it. The lava, or melted rock, would be

Fig. 39.

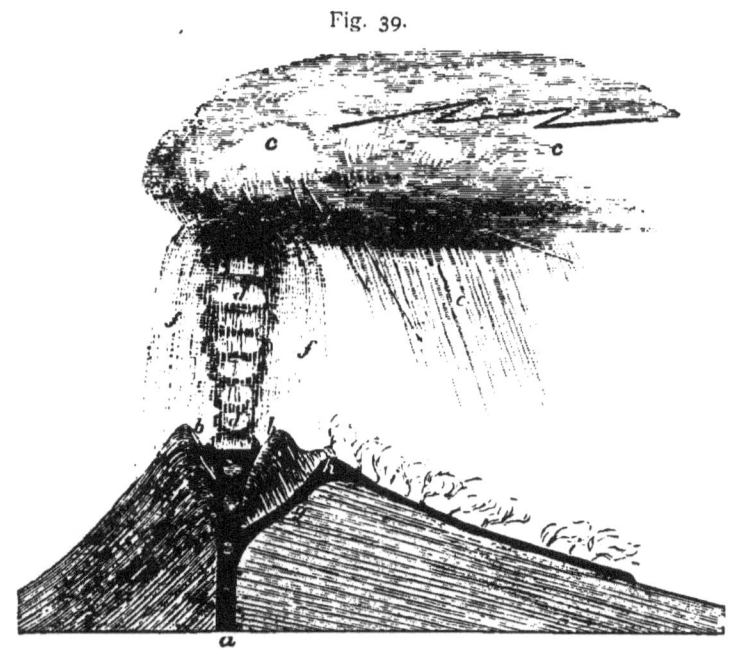

Diagrammatic section of an active volcano.

a, Central pipe or funnel.   *b*, *b*, Walls of the crater or cup.   *c*, *c*, Dark turbid cloud formed by the ascending globular clouds *d*, *d*.   *e*, Rain-shower from escaped vapour.   *f*, *f*, Shower of blocks, cooled bombs, stones, and ashes falling back on to the cone.   *g*, Lava escaping through a fissure, and pouring out of a cone opened in the mountain side.

in much the same state as melted iron-slag is, in the huge blast-furnaces in which iron-rock is fused, only it would have floating in it great blocks of solid rock, and rounded stones called bombs which have been formed from pieces of half-melted rock whirled in air and falling back into the crater, together with clinkers or scoriæ, dust and sand, all torn off and ground down from the walls of the funnel up which the rush was coming. And in the pipe of melted rock, forcing the lava upwards, enormous bubbles of steam and gas d, d would be rising up one after another as bubbles rise in any thick boiling substances, such as boiling sugar or tar.

In the morning before the eruption, when only a little smoke was issuing from the crater, these bubbles rose very slowly through the loaded funnel and the half-cooled lava in the basin, and the booming noise, like that of heavy cannon, heard from time to time, was caused by the bursting of one of these globes of steam at the top of the funnel, as it brought up with it a feeble shower of stones, dust, and scoriæ. Meanwhile the lava surging below was forcing a passage g for itself in a weak part of the mountain-side and, just at the time when our attention was called to Vesuvius, the violent pressure from below rent open a mouth or crater at h, so that the lava began to flow down the mountain in a steady stream. This, relieving the funnel, enabled the huge steam bubbles d, d to rise more quickly, and to form the large whitish-grey cloud c, into which from time to time the red-hot blocks, scoriæ, and pumice were thrown up by the escaping steam and gases. These blocks and fragments then fell back again in a fiery shower f, f either into the cup, to be thrown up again by the bursting of the next bubble, or on to the sides of the cone, making it both broader and higher.

Only one feature in the diagram was fortunately absent the evening we went up, namely, the rain-shower *e*. The night, as I said, was calm, and the air dry, and the steam floated peacefully away. The next night, however, when many people hurried down from Rome to see the sight they were wofully disappointed, for rain-showers fell heavily from the cloud, bringing down with them the dust and ashes, which covered the unfortunate sight-seers.

This was what happened during the eruption, and the result after a few days was that the cone was a little higher, with a fresh layer of rough slaggy scoriæ on its slopes, and that on the side of the mountain behind the Hermitage a new lava stream was added to the many which have flowed there of late years. What then can we learn from this stream about the materials which come up out of the depths of the earth, and of the manner in which volcanic rocks are formed?

The lava as I saw it when coming first out of the newly-opened crater is, as I have said, like white-hot iron slag, but very soon the top becomes black and solid, a hard cindery mass full of holes and cavities with rough edges, caused by the steam and sulphur and other gases breaking through it.[1] In fact, there are so many holes and bubbles in it that it is very light and floats on the top of the heavier lava below, falling over it on to the mountain-side when it comes to the end of the stream. Still, however, the great mass moves on, so that the stream

---

[1] For the cindery nature of the surface of such a stream see the initial letter of this chapter.

11

slides over these fallen clinkers or scoriæ.   Thus
after an eruption a new flow consists of three layers ; at
the top the cooled and broken crust of clinkers, then

Fig. 40.

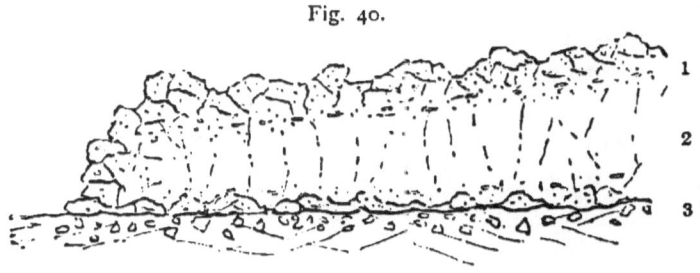

Section of a lava-flow.   (J. Geikie.)
1, Slaggy crust, formed chiefly of scoriæ of a glassy nature.   2, Middle
portion where crystals form.   3, Slaggy crust which has slipped down and
been covered by the flow.

the more solid lava, which often remains hot for years,
and lastly another cindery layer beneath, formed of
the scoriæ which have fallen from above (see Fig. 40).

   You would be surprised to see how quickly the top
hardens, so that you can actually walk across a
stream of lava a day or two after it comes out from
the mountain.   But you must not stand still or
your shoes would soon be burnt, and if you break the
crust with a stick you will at once see the red-hot
lava below ; while after a few days the cavities become
filled with crystals of common salt, sulphur or soda,
as the vapour and gases escape.

   Then as time goes on the harder minerals gradually crystallise out of the melted mass, and iron-
pyrites, copper-sulphate, and numerous other forms of
crystal appear in the lower part of the stream.   In
the clinkers above, where the cooling goes on very

rapidly, the lavas formed are semi-transparent and look much like common bottle-glass.   In fact, if you take this piece of obsidian or vol-canic glass in your hand, you might think that it had come out of an ordinary glass manufactory and had nothing re-markable in it.

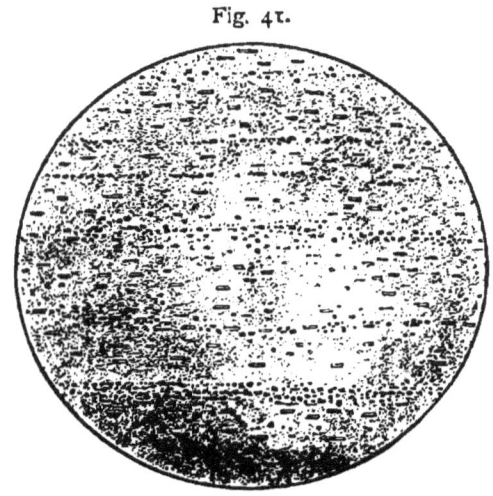

Fig. 41.

A slice of volcanic glass showing the lines of crystallites and microliths which are the be-ginnings of crystals.[1] (J. Geikie.)

But the micro-scope tells another tale.   I have put a thin slice under the first micro-scope, and this diagram (Fig. 41) shows what you will see.   Nothing, you say, but a few black specks and some tiny dark rods. True, but these specks and rods are the first be-ginnings of crystals forming out of the ground-mass of glassy lava as it cools down.   They are not real crystals, but the first step toward them, and by a careful examination of glassy lavas which have cooled at different rates, they have been seen under the microscope in all stages of growth, gradually building up different crystalline forms.   When we remember how rapidly the top of many glassy lavas cool down we can under-

---

[1] This arrangement in lines is called *fluidal structure* in lava.

stand that they have often only time to grow
very small.

The smaller specks are called *crystallites*, the
rods are called *microliths*.[1] Under the next microscope you can see the microliths much more distinctly (Fig. 42) and observe that they grow in very
regular shapes.

Our first slice, however (Fig. 41), tells us something more of their history, for the fact that they are
arranged in lines
shows that they
have grown while
the lava was flow-
ing and carrying
them along in
streams. You
will notice that
each one has its
greatest length in
the direction of
the lines, just as
pieces of stick
are carried along
lengthways in a
river. In the
second specimen

Fig. 42.

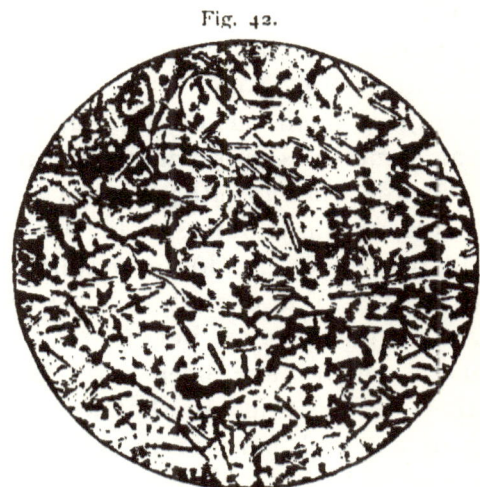

A slice of volcanic glass under the microscope,
showing well - developed microliths. (After
Cohen.)

(Fig. 42) the microliths are much larger and the
stream has evidently not been flowing fast, for they
lie in all directions.

This is what we find in the upper part of the
stream, but if we look at a piece of underlying lava

[1] *Micros*, little ; *lithos*, stone.

we find that it is much more coarse-grained, and the magnifying-glass shows many crystals in it, as well as a number of microliths.   For this lava, covered by the crust above, has remained very hot for a long time, and the crystals have had time to build themselves up out of the microliths and crystallites.

Still there is much glassy groundwork even in these lavas.   If we want to find really stony masses such as porphyry and granite made up entirely of crystals we must look inside the mountain where the molten rock is kept intensely hot for long periods, as for example in the fissure *g*, Fig. 39.

Such fissures sometimes open out on the surface like the one I saw, and sometimes only penetrate part of the way through the hill ; but in either case when the lava in them cools down, it forms solid walls called dykes which help to bind the loose materials of the mountain together.   We cannot, of course, examine these in an active volcano, but there are many extinct volcanoes which have been worn and washed by the weather for centuries, so that we can see the inside.   The dykes laid bare in the cliffs of Somma are old fissures filled with molten rock which has cooled down, and they show us many stony lavas ; and Mr. Judd tells us of one beautiful example of a ruined volcano which composes the whole island of Mull in the Hebrides, where such dykes can be traced right back to a centre.   This centre must once have been a mass of melted matter far down in the earth, and as you trace the dykes back deeper and deeper into it, the rocks grow more and more stony, till at last they are composed entirely of

large crystals closely crowded together without any glassy matter between them.   You know this crystal-
line structure well, for we have plenty of blocks of granite scattered about on Dartmoor, showing that at some time long ago molten matter must have been at work in the depths under Devonshire.

Fig. 43.

A piece of Dartmoor Granite, drawn from a specimen.

We see then that we can trace the melted rock of vol-
canoes right back — from the surface of the lava stream which cools quickly at the top, hurry-
ing the crystallites and microliths along with it — down through the volcano to the depths of the earth, where the perfect crystals form slowly and deliberately in the underground lakes of white-hot rock which are kept in a melted state at an intense heat.

But I promised you that we would have no guess-
work here, and you will perhaps ask how I can be certain what was going on in the depths when these crystals were formed.   A few years ago I could not have answered you, but now chemists, and especially two eminent French chemists, MM. Fouqué and Levy, have actually *made* lavas and shown us how it is done in Nature.

By using powerful furnaces and bellows they have succeeded in getting temperatures of all degrees, from a dazzling white heat down to a dull red, and to keep any temperature they like for a long time, so as to imitate the state of a mass of melted rock at different depths in the earth, and in this way they have actually *made* lavas in their crucibles. For example, there is a certain whitish rock common in Vesuvius called *leucotephrite*,[1] which is made up chiefly of crystals of the minerals called leucite, Labrador felspar, and augite. This they proposed to make artificially, so they took proper quantities of silica, alumina, oxide of iron, lime, potash, and soda, and putting them in a crucible, melted them by keeping them at a white heat. Then they lowered the temperature to an orange-heat, that is a heat sufficient to melt steel. They kept this heat for forty-eight hours, after which they took out some of the mixture and, letting it cool, examined a slice under the microscope. Within it they found crystals of *leucite* already formed, showing that these are the first to grow while the melted rock is still intensely hot. The rest of the mixture they kept red-hot, or at the melting-point of copper, for another forty-eight hours, and when they took it out and examined it they found that the whole of it had been transformed into microliths of the two other forms of crystals, Labrador felspar and augite, except some small eight-sided crystals of magnetite and picotite which are also found in the natural rock.

There is no need for you to remember all these names. What I do want you to remember is, that, at the different temperatures, the right crystals and beginnings of crystals grew up to form the rock which is found in Vesuvius. And what is still more

---

[1] *Leucos*, white ; *tephra*, ashes.

interesting, they grew exactly to the same stages as in the natural rock, which is composed of *crystals* of leucite and *microliths* of the two other minerals.

This is only one among numerous experiments by which we have learnt how volcanic rocks are formed and at what heat the crystals of different substances grow. We are only as yet at the beginning of this new study, and there is plenty for you boys to do by and by when you grow up. Many experiments have failed as yet to imitate certain rocks, and it is remarkable that these are usually rocks of very ancient eruptions, when *perhaps* our globe may have been in a different state to what it is now ; but this remains for us to find out.

Meanwhile I have still another very interesting slide to show you which tells us something of what is going on below the volcano. Under the third microscope I have put a slice of volcanic glass (Fig. 44) in which you will see really large crystals with dark bands curving round them. These crystals have clearly not been formed in the glass while the lava was flowing, first because they are too large to have grown up so rapidly, and secondly because they are broken at the edges in places and sometimes partly melted. They have evidently come up with the lava as it flowed out of the mountain, and the dark bands curving round them are composed of microliths which have been formed in the flow and have swept round them, as floating straws gather round a block of wood in a stream.

Such crystals as these are often found in lava streams, and in fact they make a great difference in the rate at which a stream flows, for a thoroughly melted lava shoots along at a great pace and often travels several miles in a very short time; but an imperfectly melted lava full of crystals creeps slowly along, and often does not travel far from the crater out of which it flows.

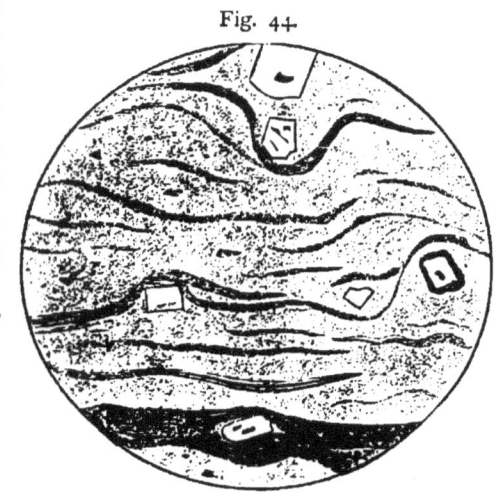

Fig. 44

So you see we have proof in this slice of volcanic glass of two separate periods of crystallisation —the period when the large

Slice of volcanic glass under the microscope, showing large included crystals brought up from inside the volcano in the fluid lava. The dark bands are lines of microliths formed as the lava cooled. (J. Geikie.)

crystals grew in the liquid mass under the mountain, and the period when the microliths were formed after it was poured out above ground. And as we know that different substances form their crystals at very different temperatures, it is not surprising that some should be able to take up the material they require and grow in the underground lakes of melted matter, even though the rest of the lava was sufficiently fluid to be forced up out of the mountain.

And here we must leave our lava stream. The microscope can tell us yet more, of marvellous tiny cavities inside the crystals, millions in a single inch, and of other crystals inside these, all of which have their history ; but this would lead us too far. We must be content for the present with having roughly traced a flow of lava from the depths below, where large crystals form in subterranean darkness, to the open air above, where we catch the tiny beginnings of crystals hardened into glassy lava before they have time to grow further.

If you will think a little for yourselves about these wonderful discoveries made with the magic-glass, you will see how many questions they suggest to us about the minerals which we find buried in the earth and running through it in veins, and you will want to know something about the more precious crystals, such as rubies, diamonds, sapphires, and garnets, and many others which Nature forms far away out of our sight. All these depend, though indirectly, upon the strange effects of underground heat, and if you have once formed a picture in your minds of what must have been going on before that magnificent lava stream crept down the mountain-side and added its small contribution to the surface of the earth, you will study eagerly all that comes in your way about crystals and minerals, and while you ask questions with the spectroscope about what is going on in the sun and stars millions of miles away, you will also ask the microscope what it has to tell of the work going on at depths many miles under your feet.

CHAPTER VI

BEFORE beginning upon the subject of our lecture to-day I want to tell you the story of a great puzzle which presented itself to me when I was a very young child. I happened to come across a little book — I can see it now as though it were yesterday—a small square green book called *World without End*, which had upon the cover a little gilt picture of a stile with trees on each side of it. That was all. I do not know what the book was about, indeed I am almost sure I never opened it or saw it again, but that stile and the title "World without End" puzzled me terribly. What was on the other side of the stile? If I could cross over it and go on and on should I be in a world which had no ending, and what would be on the other side? But then there could be no other side if it was a world without any end. I was very young, you must remember, and I grew confused and bewildered as I imagined myself reaching onwards and onwards beyond that stile and never, never resting. At last I consulted my greatest friend, an old man who did the weeding in my father's garden, and whom I believed to be very wise. He looked at first almost as bewildered as I was, but at last light dawned upon him. "I tell you what it is, Master Arthur," said he, "I do not rightly know what happens when there is no end, but I do know that there is a mighty lot to be found out in this world, and I'm thinking we had better learn first all about that, and perhaps it may teach us something which will help us to understand the other."

I daresay you will wonder what this anecdote can have to do with a lecture on the sun—I will tell you. Last night I stood on the balcony and looked out far and farther away into the star-depths of the midnight sky, marvelling what could be the history of those countless suns of which we see ever more and more as we increase the power of our telescopes, or catch the faint beams of those we cannot see and make them print their image on the photographic plate. And, as I grew oppressed at the thought of this never-ending expanse of suns and at my own littleness, I remembered all at once the little square book of my childish days with its gilt stile, and my old friend's advice to learn first all we can of that which lies nearest.

So to-day, before we travel away to the stars, we had better inquire what is known about the one star in the heavens which is comparatively near to us, our own glorious sun, which sends us all our light and heat, causes all the movements of our atmosphere, draws up the moisture from the ground to return in refreshing rain, ripens our harvests, awakens the seeds and sleeping plants into vigorous growth, and in a word sustains all the energy and life upon our earth. Yet even this star, which is more than a million times as large as our earth, and bound so closely to us that a convulsion on its surface sends a thrill right through our atmosphere, is still so far off that it is only by questioning the sunbeams it sends to us, that we can know anything about it.

You have already learnt [1] a good deal as to the size, the intense heat and light, and the photographic power of the sun, and also how his white beams of light are composed of countless coloured rays which we can separate in a prism. Now let us pass on to the more difficult problem of the nature of the sun itself, and what we know of the changes and commotions going on in that blazing globe of light.

We will try first what we can see for ourselves. If you take a card and make a pin-hole in it, you can look through this hole straight at the sun without injuring your eye, and you will see a round shining disc on which, perhaps, you may detect a few dark spots. Then if you take your hand telescopes, which I have shaded by putting a piece of smoked glass inside the eye-piece, you will find that this shining disc is really a round globe, and moreover, although the object-glass of your telescopes measures

[1] *Fairyland of Science*, Chapter II.

12

only two-and-a-half inches across, you will be able to see the dark spots very distinctly and to observe that they are shaded, having a deep spot in the centre with a paler shadow round it.

As, however, you cannot all use the telescopes, and those who can will find it difficult to point them truly on to the sun, we will adopt still another plan. I will turn the object-glass of my portable telescope

Fig. 45.

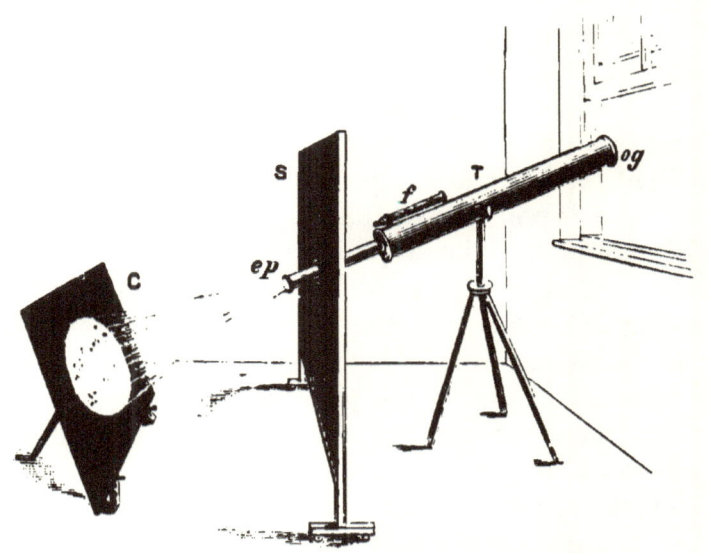

Face of the sun projected on a sheet of cardboard C.
T, Telescope. *f,* Finder. *og,* Object-glass. *ep,* Eye-piece. S, Screen shutting off the diffused light from the window.

full upon the sun's face, and bringing a large piece of cardboard on an easel near to the other end, draw it slowly backward till the eye-piece forms a clear sharp image upon it (see Fig. 45). This you can all see clearly, especially as I have passed the eye-piece of the telescope through a large screen *s*, which shuts off the light from the window.

You have now an exact image of the face of the sun and the few dark spots which are upon it, and we have brought, as it were, into our room that great globe of light and heat which sustains all the life and vigour upon our earth.

This small image can, however, tell us very little. Let us next see what photography can show us. The diagram (Fig. 46) shows a photograph of the sun taken by Mr. Selwyn in October 1860. Let me describe how this is done. You will remember that there is a point in the telescope tube where the rays of light form a real image of the object at which the telescope is pointed (see p. 44). Now an astronomer who wishes to take a photograph of the sun takes away the eye-piece of his telescope and puts a photographic plate in the tube exactly at the place where this real image is formed. He takes care to blacken the frame of the plate and shuts up this end of the telescope and the plate in a completely dark box, so that no diffused light from outside can reach it. Then he turns his telescope upon the sun that it may print its image.

But the sun's light is so strong that even in a second of time it would print a great deal too much, and all would be black and confused. To prevent this he has a strip of metal which slides across the tube of the telescope in front of the plate, and in the upper part of this strip a very fine slit is cut. Before he begins, he draws the metal up so that the slit is outside the

tube and the solid portion within, and he fastens it
in this position by a thread drawn through and tied
to a bar outside.   Then he turns his telescope on the
sun, and as soon as he wishes to take the photograph
he cuts the thread.   The metal slides across the
tube with a flash, the slit passing across it and out
again below in the hundredth part of a second, and

Fig. 46.

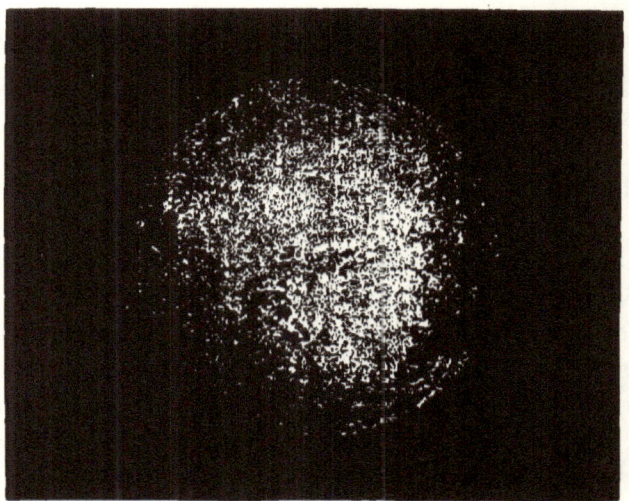

Photograph of the face of the sun, taken by Mr. Selwyn. October 1800,
showing spots, faculæ, and mottled surface.

in that time the sun has printed through the slit the
picture before you.

In it you will observe at least two things not
visible on our card-image.   The spots, though in a
different position from where we see them to-day,
look much the same, but round them we see also
some bright streaks called *faculæ*, or torches, which

often appear in any region where a spot is forming, while the whole face of the sun appears mottled with bright and darker spaces intermixed. Those of you who have the telescopes can see this mottling quite distinctly through them if you look at the sun. The bright points have been called by many names, and are now generally known as " light granules," as good a name, perhaps, as any other.

This is all our photograph can tell us, but the round disc there shown, which is called the *photosphere*, or light-giving sphere, is by no means the whole of the sun, though it is all we see daily with the naked eye. Whenever a total eclipse of the sun takes place— by the dark body of the moon coming between us and it, so as to shut out the whole of this disc—a brilliant white halo, called the crown or *corona*, is seen to extend for many thousands of miles all round the darkened globe. It varies very much in shape, sometimes forming a kind of irregular square, sometimes a circle with off-shoots, as in Fig. 47, which shows what Major Tennant saw in India during the total eclipse of August 18, 1868, and at other times it shoots out in long pearly white jets and sheets of light with dark spaces between. On the whole it varies periodically. At the time of few sun-spots its extensions are equatorial ; but when the sun's face is much covered with spots, they are diagonal, stretching away from the spot-zones, but not nearly so far.

And besides this corona there are seen very curious flaming projections on the edge of the sun, which begin to appear as soon as the moon covers the bright disc. In our diagram (Fig. 47) you see them

on the left side where the moon is just creeping over
the limits of the photosphere and shutting out the
strong light of the sun as the eclipse becomes total.
A very little later they are better seen on the other

Fig. 47.

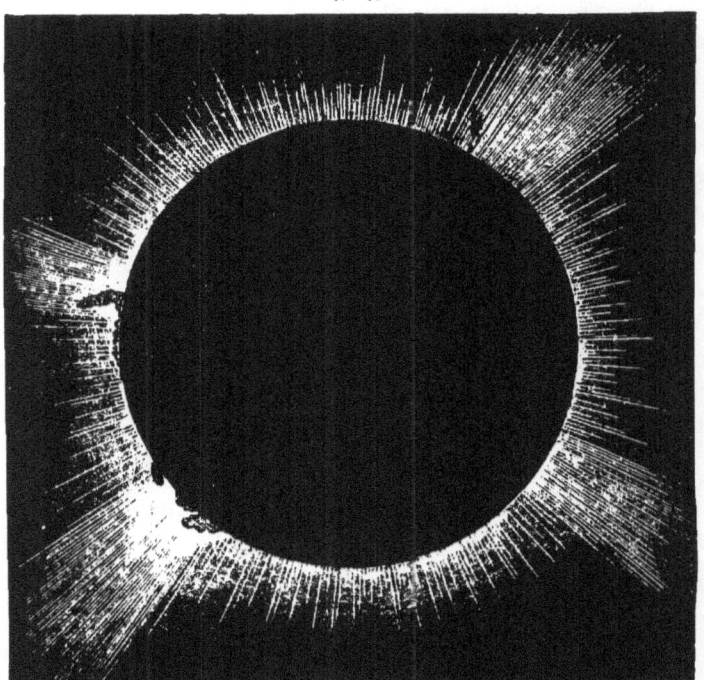

Total eclipse of the sun, as drawn by Major Tennant at Guntoor in India,
August 18, 1868, showing corona and the protuberances seen at the
beginning of totality.

side just before the bright edge of the sun is uncovered as the moon passes on its way.   These projections in the real sun are of a bright red colour, and
they take on all manners of strange shapes, sometimes

looking like ranges of fiery hills, sometimes like gigantic spikes and scimitars, sometimes even like branching fiery trees.. They were called *prominences* before their nature was well understood, and will probably always keep that name. It would be far better, however, if some other name such as "glowing clouds" or "red jets" could be used, for there is now no doubt that they are jets of gases, chiefly hydrogen, constantly playing over the face of the sun, though only seen when his brighter light is quenched. They have been found to shoot up 20,000, 80,000, and even as much as 350,000 miles beyond the edge of the shining disc ; and this last means that the flames were so gigantic that if they had started from our earth they would have reached beyond the moon. We shall see presently that astronomers are now able by the help of the spectroscope to see the prominences even when there is no eclipse, and we know them to be permanent parts of the bright globe.

This gives us at last the whole of the sun, so far as we know. There is, indeed, a strange faint zodiacal light, a kind of pearly glow seen after sunset or before sunrise extending far beyond the region of the corona ; but we understand so little about this that we cannot be sure that it actually belongs to the sun.

And now how shall I best give you an idea of what little we do know about this great surging monster of light and heat which shines down upon us ? You must give me all your attention, for I want to make the facts quite clear, that you may take a firm hold upon them.

Our first step is to question the sunlight which comes to us ; and this we do with the spectroscope. Let me remind you how we read the story of light through this instrument. Taking in a narrow beam of light through a fine slit, we pass the beam through a lens to make the rays parallel, and then throw it upon a prism or row of prisms, so that each set of waves of coloured light coming through the slit is bent on its own road and makes an upright image of the slit on any screen or telescope put to receive it (see Fig. 21, p. 52). Now when the light we examine comes from a glowing solid-like white-hot iron, or a glowing liquid, or a gas under such enormous pressure that it behaves like a liquid, then the images of the slit always overlap each other, so that we see a continuous unbroken band of colour. However much you spread out the light you can never break up or separate the spectrum in any part.[1] But when you send the light, of a glowing gas such as hydrogen through the spectroscope, or of a substance melted into gas or vapour, such as sodium or iron vaporised by great heat, then it is a different story. Such gases give only a certain number of bright lines quite separate from each other on the dark background, and each kind of gas gives its own peculiar lines ; so that even when several are glowing together there is no confusion, but when you look at them through the spectroscope you can detect the presence of each gas by its own lines in the spectrum.

To make quite sure of this we will close the

[1] Two rare earths, Erbia and Didymium, form an exception to this, but they do not concern us here.

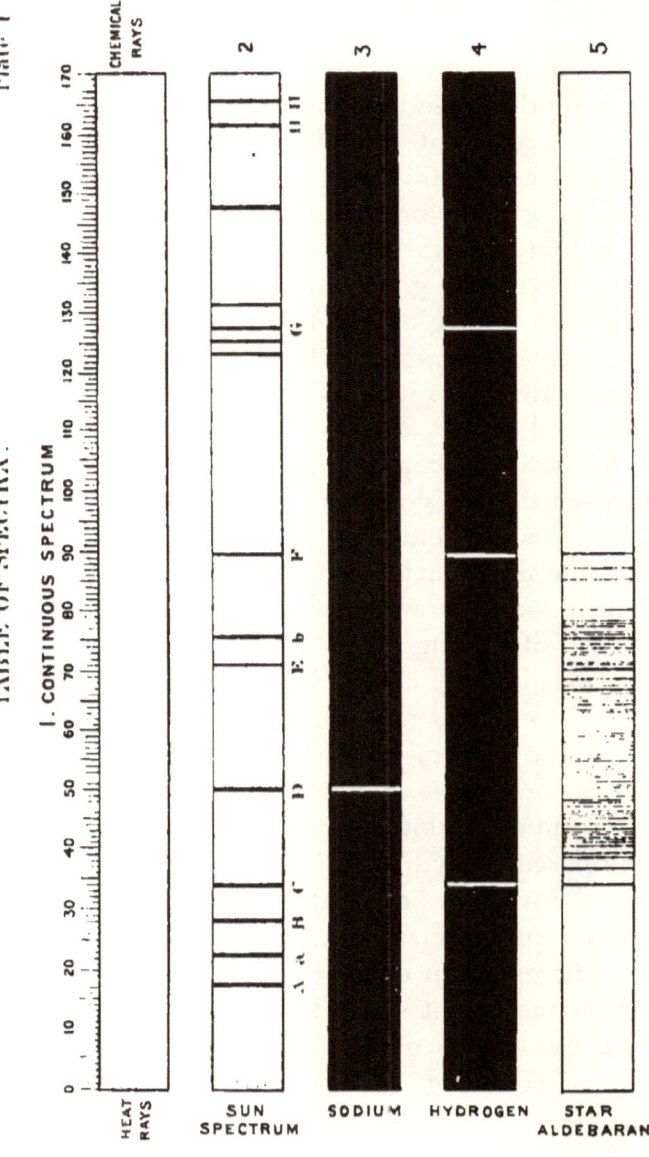

TABLE OF SPECTRA.

Plate. I

CHEMICAL RAYS

I. CONTINUOUS SPECTRUM

HEAT RAYS

SUN SPECTRUM

SODIUM

HYDROGEN

STAR ALDEBARAN

shutters and put a pinch of salt in a spirit-flame. Salt is chloride of sodium, and in the flame the sodium glows with a bright yellow light. Look at this light through your small direct-vision spectroscopes [1] and you see at once the bright yellow double-line of sodium (No. 3, Plate I.) start into view across the faint continuous spectrum given by the spirit-flame. Next I will show you glowing hydrogen. I have here a glass tube containing hydrogen, so arranged that by connecting two wires fastened to it with the induction coil of our electric battery it will soon glow with a bright red colour. Look at this through your spectroscopes and you will see three bright lines, one red, one greenish blue, and one indigo blue, standing out on the dark background (No. 4, Plate I.)

Think for a moment what a grand power this gives you of reading as in a book the different gases which are glowing in the sky even billions of miles away. You would never mistake the lines of hydrogen for the line of sodium, but when looking at a nebula or any mass of glowing gas you could say at once "sodium is glowing there," or "that cloud must be composed of hydrogen."

Now, opening the shutters, look at the sunlight through your spectroscopes. Here you have something different from either the continuous spectrum of solids, or the bright separate lines of gases, for while you have a bright-coloured band you have also some dark lines crossing it (No. 2, Plate I.) It is those

[1] A direct-vision spectroscope is like a small telescope with prisms arranged inside the tube. The object-glass end is covered by two pieces of metal, which slide backwards and forwards by means of a screw, so that a narrow or broad slit can be opened.

dark lines which enable us to guess what is going on in the sun before the light comes to us.   In 1859 Professor Kirchhoff made an experiment which explained those dark lines, and we will repeat it now. Take a good look at the sunlight spectrum, to fix the lines in your memory, and then close the shutters again.

I have here our magic-lantern with its lime-light,

Fig. 48.

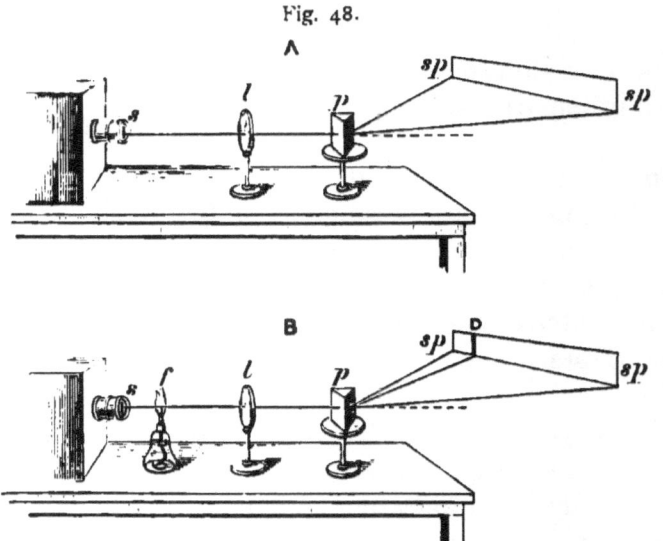

Kirchhoff's experiment, explaining the dark lines in sunlight.
A, Limelight dispersed through a prism.   s, Slit through which the beam of light comes. l, Lens bringing it to a focus on the prism p.   sp, Continuous spectrum thrown on the wall. B, The same light, with the flame f containing glowing sodium placed in front of it.   D, Dark sodium line appearing in the spectrum.

in which the solid lime glows with a white heat, in consequence of the jets of oxygen and hydrogen burning round it. This was the light Kirchhoff used, and you know it will give a continuous bright band in the spectroscope. I put a cap with a narrow slit in it over the lantern tube, so as to get a narrow beam of light ; in front of this I put a lens *l*, and in front of this again the prism *p*. The slit and the prism act exactly like your spectroscopes, and you can all see the continuous spectrum on the screen (*sp*, A, Fig. 48). Next I put a lighted lamp of very weak spirit in front of the slit, and find that it makes no difference, for whatever light it gives only strengthens the spectrum. But now notice carefully. I am going to put a little salt into the flame, and you would expect that the sodium in it, when turned to glowing vapour, causing it to look yellow, would strengthen the yellow part of the spectrum and give a bright line. This is what Kirchhoff expected, but to his intense surprise he saw as you do now a *dark line* D start out where the bright line should have been.

What can have happened ? It is this. The oxy-hydrogen light is very hot indeed, the spirit flame with the sodium is comparatively weak and cool. So when those special coloured waves of the oxyhydrogen light which agree with those of the sodium light reached the flame, they spent all their energy in heating up those waves to their own temperature, and while all the other coloured rays travelled on and reached the screen, these waves were stopped or *absorbed* on the way, and consequently there was a blank, black space in the spectrum where they should have been. If I could put a hydrogen flame cooler than the original light in the road, then there would be three dark lines where the bright hydrogen lines should be, and so with every other gas. *The cool vapour in front of the hot light cuts off from the white ray exactly those waves which it gives out itself when burning.*

Thus each black line of the sun-spectrum (No. 2, Plate I.), tells us that some particular ray of sunlight has been absorbed by a cooler vapour *of its own kind* somewhere between the sun and us, and it must be in the sun itself, for when we examine other stars we often find dark lines in their spectrum different from those in the sun, and this shows that the missing rays must have been stopped close at home, for if they were stopped in our atmosphere they would all be alike.

There are, by the bye, some lines which we know are caused by our atmosphere, especially when it is full of invisible water vapour, and these we easily detect, because they show more distinctly when the sun is low and shines through a thicker layer of air than when he is high up and shines through less.

But to return to the sun. In your small spectroscopes you see very few dark lines, but in larger and more perfect ones they can be counted by thousands, and can be compared with the bright lines of glowing gases burnt here on earth. In the spectrum of glowing iron vapour 460 lines are found to agree with dark lines in the sun-spectrum, and other gases have nearly as many. Still, though thousands of lines can now be explained, by matching them with the bright lines of known gases, the whole secret of sunlight is not yet solved, for the larger number of lines still remain a riddle to be read.

We see then that the spectroscope teaches us that the round light-giving disc or photosphere of the sun consists of a bright and intensely hot light shining behind a layer of cooler though still very hot vapours, which form a kind of shell of luminous clouds around it, and in this shell, or *reversing layer*—as it is often called, because it turns light to darkness—we have proved that iron, lead, copper, zinc, aluminum, magnesium, potassium, sodium, carbon, hydrogen, and many other substances common to our earth, exist in a state of vapour for a depth of perhaps 1000 miles.

You will easily understand that when the spectroscope had told so much, astronomers were eager to learn what it would reveal about the prominences or red jets seen during eclipses, and they got an answer in India during that same eclipse of August 1868 which is shown in our diagram (Fig. 47). Making use of the time during which the prominences were seen, they turned the telescope upon them with a spectroscope attached to it, and saw a number of bright lines start out, of which the chief were the three bright lines of hydrogen, showing that these curious appearances are really flames of glowing gas.

In the same year Professor Jannsen and Mr. Lockyer succeeded in seeing the bright lines of the prominences in full sunlight. This was done in a very simple way, when once it was discovered to be possible, and though my apparatus (Fig. 49) is very primitive compared with some now made, it will serve to explain the method.

When an astronomer wishes to examine the spectrum of any special part of the sun, he takes off

13

the eye-piece of his telescope and screws the spectro-

Fig. 49.

The spectroscope attached to the telescope for the examination of the sun.   (Lockyer.)

P, Pillar of Telescope.   T, Telescope.   S, Finder or small telescope for pointing the telescope in position.   *a, a, b,* Supports fastening the spectroscope to the telescope.   *d,* Collimator or tube carrying the slit at the end nearest the telescope, and a lens at the other end to render the rays parallel.   *c,* Plate on which the prisms are fixed.   *e,* Small telescope through which the observer examines the spectrum after the ray has been dispersed in the prisms.   *h,* Micrometer for measuring the relative distance of the lines.

scope upon the draw-tube.   The spectroscope is

made exactly like the large one for ordinary work. The tube *d* (Fig. 49) carries the slit at the end nearest the telescope, and this slit must be so placed as to stand precisely at the principal focus of the lens where the sun's image is formed (see *i*, *i*, p. 44). This comes to exactly the same thing as if we could put the slit close against the face of the sun, so as to show only the small strip which it covers, and by moving it to one part or another of the image we can see any point that we wish and no other. The light then passes through the tube *d* into the round of prisms standing on the tray *c*, and the observer looking through the small telescope *e* sees the spectrum as it emerges from the last prism. In this way astronomers can examine the spectrum of a spot, or part of a spot, or of a bright streak, or any other mark on the sun's face.

Now in looking at the prominences we have seen that the difficulty is caused by the sunlight, between us and them, overpowering the bright lines of the gas, nor could we overcome this if it were not for a difference which exists between the two kinds of light. The more you disperse or spread out the continuous sun-spectrum the fainter it becomes, but in spreading out the bright lines of the gas you only send them farther and farther apart; they themselves remain almost as bright as ever. So, when the telescope forms an image of the red flame in front of the slit, though the glowing gas and the sunlight both send rays into the spectroscope, you have only to use enough prisms and arrange them in such a way that the sunlight is dispersed into a very long faint spectrum, and then the bright lines of the flames will stand out bright and clear. Of course only a small part of the long spectrum can be seen at once, and the lines must be studied separately. On the other hand, if you want to compare the strong light of the sun with the bright lines of the prominences, you place the slit just at the edge of the sun's image in the telescope, so that half the slit is on the sun's face and half on the prominence. The prisms then disperse the sunlight between you and the prominences, while they only lessen the strong light of the sun itself, which still shows clearly. In this way the two spectra are seen side by side and the dark and bright lines can be compared accurately together (see Fig. 50).

Fig. 50.

Bright lines of prominences.

Sun-spectrum with dark lines.

Wherever the telescope is turned all round the sun the lines of luminous gas are seen, showing that they form a complete layer outside the photosphere, or light-giving mass, of the sun. This layer of luminous gases is called the *chromosphere*, or coloured sphere. It lies between the photosphere and the corona, and is supposed to be at least 5000 miles deep, while, as we have seen, the flames shoot up from it to fabulous heights.

The quiet red flames are found to be composed of hydrogen and another new metal called helium ; but lower down, near the sun's edge, other bright lines are seen, showing that sodium, magnesium, and other metals are there, and when violent eruptions occur these often surge up and mingle with the purer gas above. At other times the eruptions below fling the red flames aloft with marvellous force, as when Professor Young saw a long low-lying cloud of hydrogen, 100,000 miles long, blown into shreds and flung up to a height of 200,000 miles, when the fragments streamed away and vanished in two hours. Yet all these violent commotions and storms are unseen by us on earth unless we look through our magic glasses.

You will wonder no doubt how the spectroscope can show the height and the shape of the flames. I will explain to you, and I hope to show them you one day. You must remember that the telescope makes a small real image of the flame at its focus, just as in one of our earlier experiments you saw the exact image of the candle-flame upside down on the paper (see p. 33). The reason why we only see a strip of the flame in the spectroscope is because the slit is so narrow. But when once the sunlight was dispersed so as no longer to interfere, Dr. Huggins found that it is possible to open the slit wide enough to take in the image of the whole flame, and then, by turning the spectroscope so as to bring one of the bright hydrogen lines into view, the actual shape of the prominence is seen, only it will look a different colour, either red, greenish - blue, or indigo - blue, according to the line chosen. As the image of the whole sun and its appendages in the telescope is so very small, you will understand that even a very narrow slit will really take in a very large prominence several thousand miles in length. Fig 51 shows a drawing by Mr. Lockyer of a group of flames he observed

Fig. 51.

Red prominences, as drawn by Mr. Lockyer during the total eclipse of March 14, 1869.

very soon after Dr. Huggins suggested the open slit, and these shapes did not last long, for in another picture he drew ten minutes later their appearance had already changed.

These then are some of the facts revealed to us by our magic glasses. I scarcely expect you to remember all the details I have given you, but you will at least understand now how astronomers actually penetrate into the secrets of the sun by bringing its image into their observatory, as we brought it to-day on the card-board, and then making it tell its own tale through the prisms of the spectroscope ; and you will retain some idea of the central light of the sun with its surrounding atmosphere of cooler gases and its layer of luminous lambent gases playing round it beyond.

Of the corona I cannot tell you much, except that it is far more subtle than anything we have spoken of yet ; that it is always strongest when the sun is most spotted ; that it is partly made up of self-luminous gases whose bright lines we can see, especially an unknown green ray ; while it also shines partly by reflected light from the sun, for we can trace in it faint dark lines ; lastly it fades away into the mysterious zodiacal light, and so the sun ends in mystery at its outer fringe as it began at its centre.

And now at last, having learnt something of the material of the sun, we can come back to the spots and ask what is known about them. As I have said, they are not always the same on the sun's face. On the contrary, they vary very much both in number and size. In some years the sun's face is quite free from them, at others there are so many that they form two wide belts on each side of the sun's equator, with a clear space of about six degrees between. No spots ever appear near the poles. Herr Schwabe, who watched the sun's face patiently for more than thirty years, has shown that it is most spotted about every eleven years, then the spots disappear very quickly and reappear slowly till the full-spot time comes round again.

Some spots remain a very short time and then break up and disappear, but others last for days, weeks, and even months, and when we watch these, we find that a spot appears to travel slowly across the face of the sun from east to west and then round the western edge so that it disappears. It is when it reaches the edge that we can convince ourselves that the spot is really part of the sun, for there is no space to be seen between them, the edge and the spot are one, as the last trace of the dark blotch passes out of sight. In fact, it is not the spot which has crossed the sun's face, but the sun itself which has turned, like our earth, upon its axis, carrying the spot round with it. As some spots remain long enough to reappear, after about twelve or thirteen days, on the opposite edge, and even pass round two or three times, astronomers can reckon that the sun takes about twenty-five days and five hours in performing one revolution. You will wonder why I say only *about* twenty-five, but I do so because all spots do not come round in exactly the same time, those farthest from the equator lag rather more than a day behind those nearer to it, and this is explained by the layer of gases in which they are formed, drifting back in higher latitudes as the sun turns.

It is by watching a spot as it travels across the sun, that we are able to observe that the centre part lies deeper in the sun's face than the outer rim. There are many ways of testing this, and you can try one yourselves with a telescope if you watch day after day. I will explain it by a simple experiment. I have here a round lump of stiff dough, in which I have made a small hollow and blackened the bottom with a drop of ink. As I turn this round, so that the hollow facing you moves from right to left, you will see that after it passes the middle of the face, the hole appears narrower and narrower till it disappears, and if you observe carefully you will note that the dark centre is the first thing you lose sight of, while the edges of the cup are still seen, till just before the spot disappears altogether. But now I will stick a wafer on, and a pea half into, the dough, marking the centre of each with ink. Then I turn the ball again. This time you lose sight of the foremost edge first, and the dark centre is seen almost to the last moment. This shows that if the spots were either flat marks, or hillocks, on the sun's face, the dark centre would remain to the last, but as a fact it disappears before the rim. Father Secchi has tried to measure the depth of a spot-cavity, and thinks they vary from 1000 to 3000 miles deep. But there are many difficulties in interpreting the effects of light and shadow at such an enormous distance, and some astronomers still doubt whether spots are really depressions.

For many centuries now the spots have been watched forming and dispersing, and this is roughly speaking what is seen to happen. When the sun is fairly clear and there are few spots, these generally form quietly, several black dots appearing and disappearing with bright streaks or *faculæ* round their edge, till one grows bigger than the rest, and forms a large dark nucleus, round which, after a time, a half-shadow or *penumbra* is seen and we have a sun-spot com-

Fig. 52.

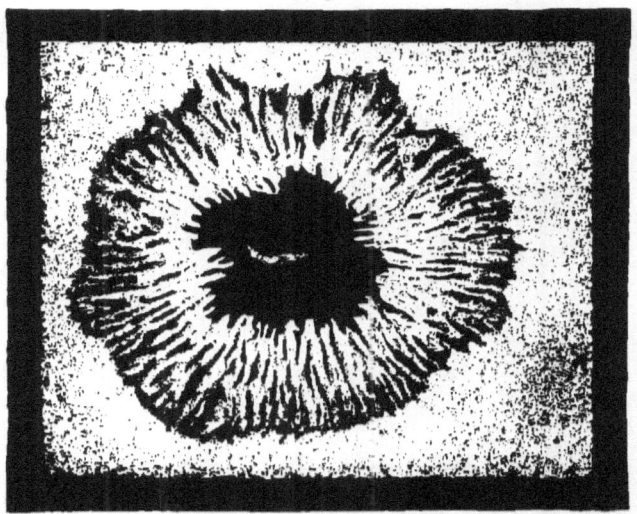

A quiet sun-spot. [Secchi.]

plete, with bright edges, dark shadow, and deep black centre (Fig. 52). This lasts for a certain time and then it becomes bridged over with light streaks, the dark spot breaks up and disappears, and last of all the half-shadow dies away.

But things do not always take place so quietly. When the sun's face is very troubled and full of spots, the bright *faculæ*, which appear with a spot, seem to heave and wave, and generally several dark centres form with whirling masses of light round them, while in some of them tongues of fire appear to leap up from below (Fig. 53). Such spots change quickly from day to day, even if they remain for a long time, until at last by degrees the dark centres become less distinct, the half-shadows disappear,

Fig. 53.

A tumultuous sun-spot. (Langley.)

leaving only the bright streaks, which gradually settle down into luminous points or *light granules.* These light granules are in fact supposed by astronomers to be the tips of glowing clouds heaving up everywhere, while the dark spaces between them are cooler currents passing downwards.

Below these clouds, no doubt, the great mass of the sun is in a violent state of heat and commotion, and when from time to time, whether suddenly or steadily, great upheavals and eruptions take place, bright flames dart up and luminous clouds gather and swell, so that long streaks or *faculæ* surge upon the face of the sun.

Now these hot gases rising up thus on all sides would leave room below for cooler gases to pour down from above, and these, as we know, would cut off, or absorb, much of the light coming from the body of the sun, so that the centre, where the down current was the strongest, would appear black even though some light would pass through. This is the best explanation we have as yet of the formation of a sun-spot, and many facts shown in the spectroscope help to confirm it, as for example the thickening of the dark lines of the spectrum when the slit is placed over the centre of a spot, and the flashing out of bright lines when an uprush of streaks occurs either across the spots or round it.

And now, before you go, I must tell you of one of these wonderful uprushes, which sent such a thrill through our own atmosphere, as to tell us very plainly the power which the sun has over our globe. The year 1859 was remarkable for sun-spots, and on September 1, when two astronomers many miles apart were examining them, they both saw, all at once, a sudden cloud of light far brighter than the general surface of the sun burst out in the midst of a group of spots. The outburst began at eight minutes past eleven in the forenoon, and in five minutes it was gone again, but in that time it had swept across a space of 35,000 miles on the sun! Now both before and after this violent outburst took place a magnetic storm raged all round the earth, brilliant auroras were seen in all parts of the world, sparks flashed from the telegraph wires, and the telegraphic signalmen at Washington and Philadelphia received severe electric shocks. Messages were interrupted, for the storm took possession of the wires and sent messages of its own, the magnetic needles darting to and fro as though seized with madness. At the very instant when the bright outburst was seen in the sun, the self-registering instruments at Kew marked how three needles jerked all at once wildly aside ; and the following night the skies were lit up with wondrous lights as the storm of electric agitation played round the earth.

We are so accustomed to the steady glow of sunshine pouring down upon us that we pay very little heed to daylight, though I hope none of us are quite so ignorant as the man who praised the moon above the sun, because it shone in the dark night, whereas the sun came in the daytime when there was light enough already ! Yet probably many of us do not actually realise how close are the links which bind us to our brilliant star as he carries us along with him through space. It is only when an unusual outburst occurs, such as I have just described, that we feel how every thrill which passes through our atmosphere, through the life-current of every plant, and through the fibre and nerve of every animal has some relation to the huge source of light, heat, electricity, and magnetism at which we are now gazing across a space of more than 93,000,000 miles. Yet it is well

14

to remember that the sudden storm and the violent eruption are the exceptional occurrences, and that their use to us as students is chiefly to lead us to understand the steady and constant thrill which, never ceasing, never faltering, fulfils the great purpose of the unseen Lawgiver in sustaining all movement and life in our little world.

CHAPTER VII

AN EVENING AMONG THE STARS

D O you love the stars ? " asked the magician of his lads, as they crowded round him on the college green, one evening in March, to look through his portable telescope. " Have you ever sat at the window on a clear frosty night, or in the garden in summer, and looked up at those wondrous lights in the sky, pondering what they are, and what purpose they serve ? "

I will confess to you that when I lived in London I did not think much about the stars, for in the streets very few can be seen at a time even on a clear night ; and during the long evenings in summer, when town people visit the country, you must stay up late to see a brilliant display of starlight. It is when driving or walking across country on a winter's evening week after week, and looking all round the sky, that the glorious suns of heaven force you to take notice of them ; and Orion becomes a com-

panion with his seven brilliant stars and his magnificent nebula, which appears as a small pale blue
patch, to eyes accustomed to look for it, when the
night is very bright and clear.   It is then that
Charles's Wain becomes quite a study in all its
different positions, its horses now careering upwards,
now plunging downwards, while the waggon, whether
upwards or downwards, points ever true, by the two
stars of its tail-board, to the steadfast pole-star.

It is on such nights as these that, looking southward
from Orion, we recognise the dog-star Sirius, bright
long before other stars have conquered the twilight,
and feast our eye upon his glorious white beams ;
and then, turning northwards, are startled by the soft
lustrous sheen of Vega just appearing above the
horizon.

But stop, I must remember that I have not yet
introduced you to these groups of stars ; and moreover
that, though we shall find them now in the positions
I mention, yet if you look for them a few hours later
to-night, or at the same hour later in the year, you
will not find them in the same places in the sky.
For as our earth turns daily on its axis, the stars
appear to alter their position hour by hour, and in
the same way as we travel yearly on our journey
round the sun, they *appear* to move in the sky month
by month.   Yet with a little practice it is easy to
recognise the principal stars, for, as it is our movement and not theirs which makes us see them in
different parts of the sky, they always remain in the
same position with regard to each other.   In a very
short time, with the help of such a book as Proctor's

Star Atlas, you could pick out all the chief constellations and most conspicuous stars for yourselves.

One of the best ways is to take note of the stars each night as they creep out one by one after sunset. If you take your place at the window to-morrow night as the twilight fades away, you will see them gradually appear, now in one part, now in another of the sky, as

> " One by one each little star
> Sits on its golden throne."

The first to appear will be Sirius or the dog-star (see Fig. 54), that pure white star which you can observe now rather low down to the south, and which belongs to the constellation *Canis Major*. As Sirius is one of the most brilliant stars in the sky, he can be seen very soon after the sun is gone at this time of year. If, however, you had any doubt as to what star he was, you would not doubt long, for in a little while two beautiful stars start into view above him more to the west, and between them three smaller ones in a close . row, forming the cross in the constellation of Orion, which is always very easy to recognise. Now the three stars of Orion's belt which make the short piece of the cross always point to Sirius, while Betelgeux in his right shoulder, and Rigel in his left foot (see Figs. 54 and 55), complete the long piece, and these all show very early in the twilight. You would have to wait longer for the other two leading stars, Bellatrix in the right shoulder and κ Orionis in the right leg, for these stars are feebler and only seen when the light has faded quite away.

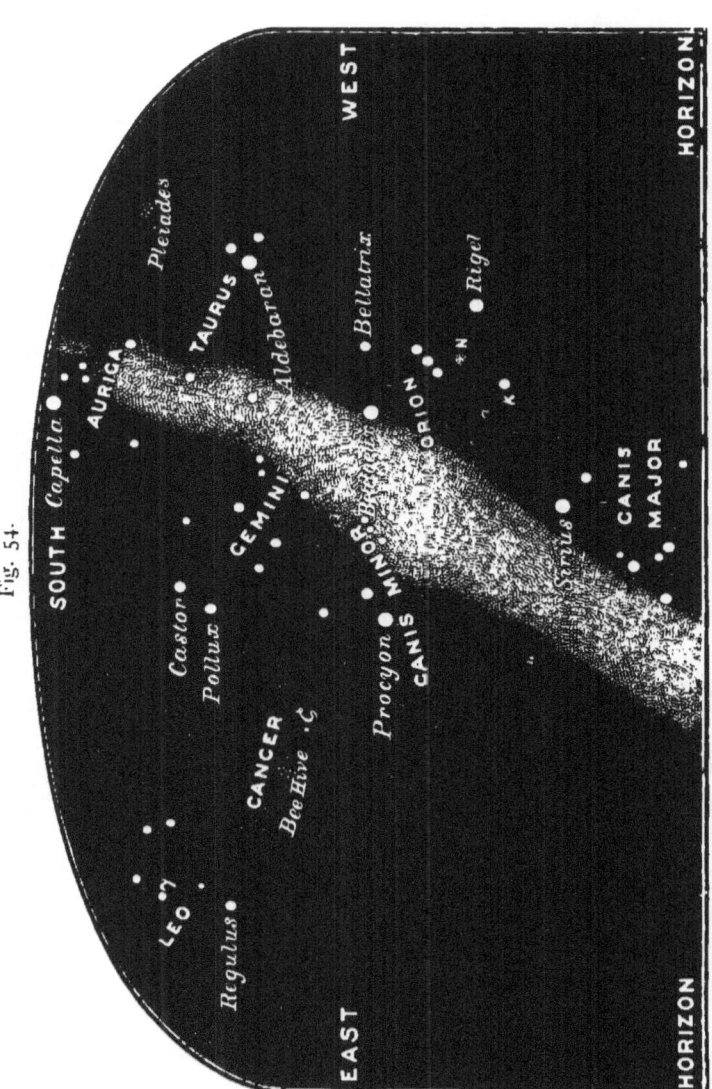

Fig. 54.

Some of the constellations seen when looking south in March from six to nine o'clock.

By that time you would see that there are an immense number of stars in Orion visible even to the naked eye, besides the veil of misty, tiny stars called the "Milky Way" which passes over his arm and club. Yet the figure of the huntsman is very difficult to trace, and the seven bright stars, the five of the cross and those in the left arm and knee, are all you need remember.

No! not altogether all, for on a bright clear night like this you can detect a faint greenish blue patch (N, Fig. 54) just below the belt, and having a bright star in the centre. This is called the "Great Nebula" or mist of Orion (see Frontispiece). With your telescopes it looks very small indeed, for only the central and brightest part is seen. Really, however, it is so widespread that our whole solar system is as nothing compared to it. But even your telescopes will show, somewhere

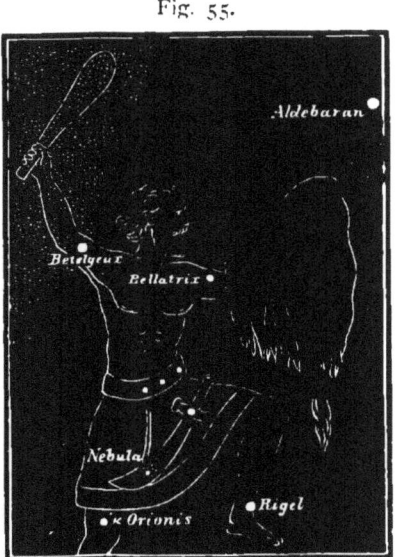

Fig. 55.

Chief stars of Orion, with Aldebaran.
(After Proctor.)

near the centre, what appears to be a bright and very beautiful star (see Fig. 55) surrounded by a darker space than the rest of the nebula, while in my telescope you will see many stars scattered over the mist.

Now first let me tell you that these last stars do

not, so far as we know, lie *in* the nebula, but are scattered about in the heavens between us and it, perhaps millions of miles nearer our earth.   But with the bright star in the centre it is different, for the spectroscope tells us that the mist passes *over* it, so that it is either behind or in the nebula. Moreover, this star is very interesting, for it is not really one star, but six arranged in a group (see Fig. 56). You can see four distinctly through my telescope, forming a trapezium or four-sided figure, and more powerful instruments show two smaller ones.   So θ Orionis, or the Trapezium of Orion, is a multiple star, probably lying in the midst of the nebula.

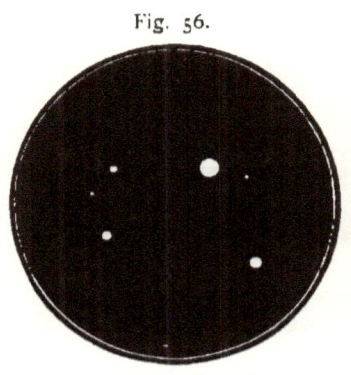

Fig. 56.

The trapezium, θ Orionis, in the nebula of Orion.   (Herschel.)

The next question is, What is the mist itself composed of?   For a long time telescopes could give us no answer.   At last one night Lord Rosse, looking through his giant telescope at the densest part of the nebula, saw myriads of minute stars which had never been seen before.   " Then," you will say, " it is after all only a cluster of stars too small for our telescopes to distinguish."   Wait a bit ; it is always dangerous to draw hasty conclusions from single observations. What Lord Rosse said was true as to that particular part of the nebula, but not the whole truth even there, and not at all true of other parts, as the spectroscope tells us.

For though the light of nebulæ, or luminous mists, is so faint that a spectrum can only be got by most delicate operations, yet Dr. Huggins has succeeded in examining several. Among these is the nebula of Orion, and we now know that when the light of the mist is spread out it gives, not a continuous band

Fig. 57.

Nebula-spectrum.

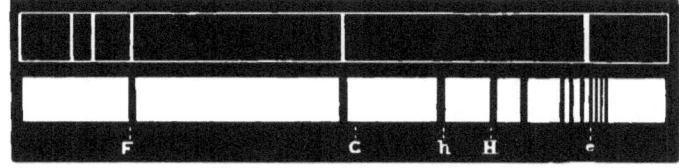

Sun-spectrum.

Spectrum of Orion's Nebula, showing bright lines, with sun-spectrum below for comparison.

of colour such as would be given by stars, but *faint coloured lines* on a dark ground (see Fig. 57). Such lines as these we have already learnt are always given by gases, and the particular bright lines thrown by Orion's nebula answer to those given by nitrogen and hydrogen, and some other unknown gases. So we learn at last that the true mist of the nebula is formed of glowing gas, while parts have probably a great number of minute stars in them.

Till within a very short time ago only those people who had access to very powerful telescopes could see the real appearance of Orion, for drawings made of it were necessarily very imperfect; but now that telescopes have been made expressly for carrying photographic appliances, even these faint mists print their own image for us.   In 1880 Professor Draper of America photographed the nebula of Orion, in March 1881 Mr. Common got a still better effect, and last year Mr. Isaac Roberts succeeded in taking the most perfect and beautiful photograph[1] yet obtained, in which the true beauty of this wonderful mist stands out clearly.   I have marked on the edge of our copy two points θ and θ', and if you follow out straight lines from these points till they meet, you will arrive at the spot where the multiple star lies.   It cannot, however, be seen here, because the plate was exposed for three hours and a half, and after a time the mist prints itself so densely as to smother the light of the stars.   Look well at this photograph when you go indoors and fix it on your memory, and then on clear nights accustom your eye to find the nebula below the three stars of the belt, for it tells a wonderful story.

More than a hundred years ago the great German philosopher Kant suggested that our sun, our earth, and all the heavenly bodies might have begun as gases, and the astronomer Laplace taught this as the most likely history of their formation.   After a few years, however, when powerful telescopes showed that many of the nebulæ were only clusters of very minute stars, astronomers thought that Laplace's teaching had been wrong. But now the spectroscope has revealed to us glowing

---

[1] Reproduced in the Frontispiece with Mr. Roberts's kind permission.   The star-halo at the top of the plate is caused by diffraction of light in the telescope, and comes only from an ordinary star.

gas actually filling large spaces in the sky, and every year accurate observations and experiments tell us more and more about these marvellous distant mists. Some day, though perhaps not while you or I are here to know it, Orion's nebula, with its glowing gas and minute star-dust, may give some clue to the early history of the heavenly bodies ; and for this reason I wish you to recognise and ponder over it, as I have often done, when it shines down on the rugged moor in the stillness of a clear frosty winter's night.

But we must pass on for, while I have been talking, the whole sky has become bespangled with hundreds of stars. That glorious one to the west, which you can find by following (Fig. 54) a curved line upwards from Betelgeux, is the beautiful red star Aldebaran or the hindmost ; so called by the Arabs, because he drives before him that well-known cluster, the Pleiades, which we reach by continuing the curve westwards and upwards. Stop to look at this cluster through your telescopes, for it will delight you ; even with the naked eye you can count from six to ten stars in it, and an opera-glass will show about thirty, though they are so scattered you will have to move the glass about to find them. Yet though my telescope shows a great many more, you cannot even count all the chief ones through it, for in powerful telescopes more than 600 stars have been seen in the single cluster! while a photograph taken by Mr. Roberts shows also four lovely patches of nebula.

And now from the Pleiades let us pass on directly overhead to the beautiful star Capella, which once was red but now is blue, and drop down gently to the south-east, where Castor and Pollux, the two most prominent stars in the constellation "Gemini" or the twins, show brilliantly against the black sky. Pause here a moment, for I want to tell you something about Castor, the one nearest to Capella. If you look at Castor through your telescopes, some of you may possibly guess that it is really two stars, but you will have to look through mine to see it clearly. These two stars have been watched carefully for many years, and there is now no doubt that one of them is moving slowly round the other. Such stars as these are called "binary," to distinguish them from stars that merely *appear* double because they stand nearly in a line one behind the other in the heavens, although they may be millions of miles apart. But "binary" stars are actually moving in one system, and revolve round each other as our earth moves round the sun.

I wonder if it strikes you what a grand discovery this is? You will remember that it is gravitation which keeps the moon held to the earth so that it moves round in a circle, and which keeps the earth and other planets moving round the sun. But till these binary stars were discovered we had no means of guessing that this law had any force beyond our own solar system. Now, however, we learn that the same law and order which reigns in our small group of planets is in action billions of miles away among distant suns, so that they are held together and move round each other as our earth moves round our sun. I will repeat to you what Sir R. Ball, the Astronomer-Royal of Ireland, says about this, for his words have remained in my mind ever since I read them, and I should like them to linger in yours till you are old enough to feel their force and grandeur. " This discovery," he writes, " gave us knowledge we could have gained from no other source. From the binary stars came a whisper across the vast abyss of space. That whisper told us that the law of gravitation is not peculiar to the solar system. It gives us grounds for believing that it is obeyed throughout the length, the breadth, the depth, and the height of the entire universe."[1]

And now, leaving Castor and going round to the east, we pass through the constellation Leo or the Lion, and I want you particularly to notice six stars in the shape of a sickle, which form the front part of the lion, the brightest, called Regulus, being the end of the handle.[2] This sickle is very interesting, because it marks the part of the heavens from which the brilliant shower of November meteors radiates once in thirty-three years. This is, however, too long a story to be told to-night, so we will pass through Leo, and turning northwards, look high up in the north-east (Fig. 58), where " Charles's Wain " stretches far across the sky. I need not point this out to you, for every country lad knows and delights in it. You could not have seen it in the twilight when Sirius first shone out, for these stars are not so powerful as he is. But they come out very soon after him, and when once fairly bright, the four stars which form the waggon, wider at the top than at the

---

[1] *The Story of the Heavens.*
[2] In Fig. 54 the sickle alone comes within the picture.

13

Fig. 58.

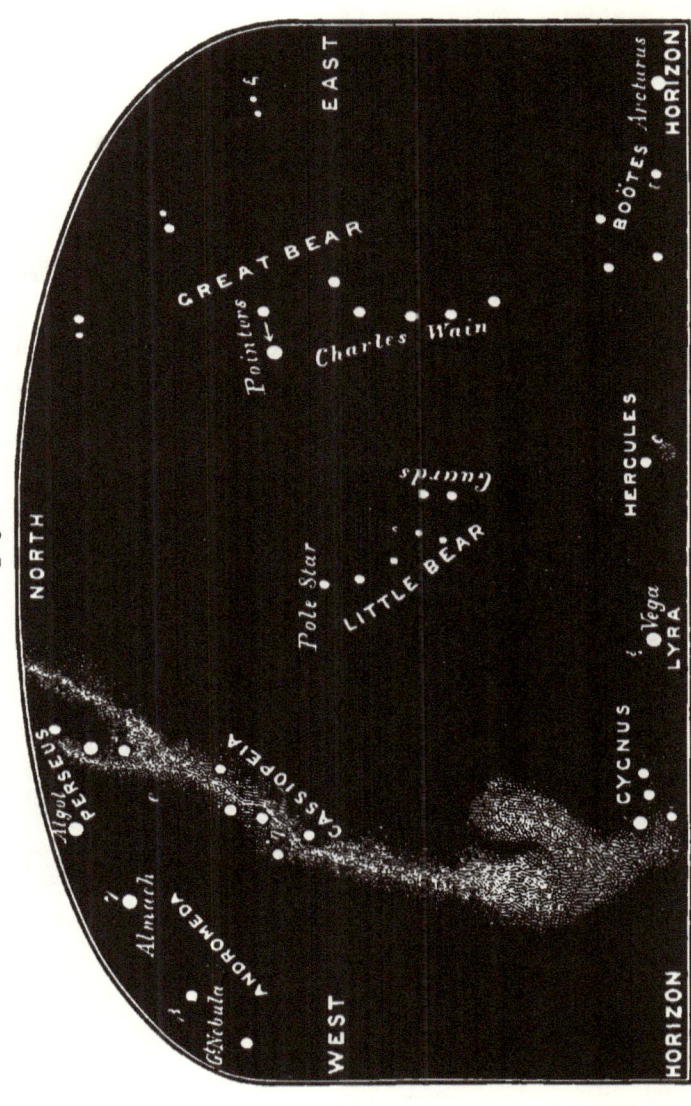

Some of the constellations seen when looking north in March from six to nine o'clock.

bottom, can never be mistaken, and the three stars in front, the last bending below the others, are just in the right position for the horses. For this reason I prefer the country people's name of Charles's Wain or Waggon to that of the "Plough," which astronomers generally give to these seven stars. They really form part of an enormous constellation called the "Great Bear" (Fig. 59), but, as in the case of Orion, it is very difficult to make out the whole of Bruin in the sky.

Now, although most people know Charles's Wain when they see it, we may still learn a good deal

Fig. 59.

The Great Bear, showing the position of Charles's Wain, and also the small binary star ζ, in the tail of whose close period has been determined.

about it. Look carefully at the second star from the waggon and you will see another star close to it, called by country people "Jack by the second horse," and by astronomers "Alcor." Even in your small telescopes you can see that Jack or Alcor is not so close as he appears to the naked eye, but a long way off from the horse, while in my telescope you will find this second horse (called Mizar) split up into two stars, one a brilliant white and the other a pale emerald green. We do not know whether these two form a binary, for they have not yet been observed to move round each other.

Take care in looking that you do not confuse the stars one with another, for you must remember that your telescope makes objects appear upside down, and Alcor will therefore appear in it *below* the two stars forming the horse.

But though we do not know whether Mizar is binary, there is a little star a long way below the waggon, in the left hind paw of the Great Bear (ξ, Figs. 58 and 59), which has taught us a great deal, for it is composed of two stars, one white and the other grey, which move right round each other once in sixty years, so that astronomers have observed more than one revolution since powerful telescopes were invented. You will have to look in my telescope to see the two stars divided, but you can make an interesting observation for yourselves by comparing the light of this binary star with the light of Castor, for Castor is such an immense distance from us that his light takes more than a hundred years to reach us, while the light of this smaller star comes in sixty-one years, yet see how incomparably brighter Castor is of the two. This proves that brilliant stars are not always the nearest, but that a near star may be small and faint and a far-off one large and bright.

There is another very interesting fact known to us about Charles's Wain which I should like you to remember when you look at it. This is that the seven stars are travelling onwards in the sky, and not all in the same direction. It was already suspected centuries ago that, besides the *apparent* motion of all the stars in the heavens caused by our own movements, they have each also a *real* motion and are travelling in space, though they are so inconceivably far off that we do not notice it. It has now been proved, by very accurate observations with powerful instruments, that three of the stars forming the waggon and the two horses

Fig. 60

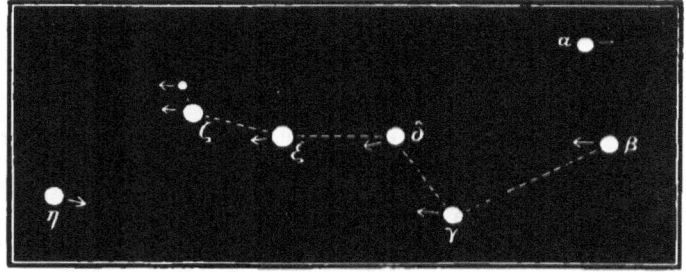

The seven stars of Charles's Wain, showing the directions in which they are travelling. (After Proctor.)

nearest to it, together with Jack, are drifting forwards (see Fig. 60), while the top star of the tailboard of the waggon and the leader of the horses are drifting the other way. Thus, thousands of years hence

Charles's Wain will most likely have quite altered its shape, though so very slowly that each generation will think it is unchanged.

One more experiment with Charles's Wain, before we leave it, will help you to imagine the endless millions of stars which fill the universe. Look up at the waggon and try to count how many stars you can see inside it with the naked eye. You may, if your eye is keen, be able to count twelve. Now take an opera-glass and the twelve become two hundred. With your telescopes they will increase again in number. In my telescope upstairs the two hundred become hundreds, while in one of the giant telescopes, such as Lord Rosse's in Ireland, or the great telescope at Washington in the United States, thousands of stars are brought into view within that four-sided space!

Now this part of the sky is not fuller of stars than many others ; yet at first, looking up as any one might on a clear evening, we thought only twelve were there. Cast your eyes all round the heavens. On a clear night like this you may perhaps, with the naked eye, have in view about 3000 stars ; then consider that a powerful telescope can multiply these by thousands upon thousands, so that we can reckon about 20,000,000 where you see only 3000. If you add to these the stars that rise later at night, and those of the southern hemisphere which never rise in our latitude, you would have in all about 50,000,000 stars, which we are able to see from our tiny world through our most powerful telescopes.

But we can go farther yet. When our telescopes fail, we turn to our other magic seer, the photographic camera, and trapping rays of light from stars invisible in the most powerful telescope, make them print their image on the photographic plate, and at once our numbers are so enormously increased that if we could photograph the whole of the heavens as visible from our earth, we should have impressions of at least 170,000,000 stars !

These numbers are so difficult to grasp that we had better pass on to something easier, and our next step brings us to the one star in the heavens which never appears to move, as our world turns. To find it we have only to draw a line upwards through the two stars in the tailboard of the waggon and on into space. Indeed these two stars are called "the Pointers," because a line prolonged onwards from them will, with a very slight curve, bring us to the "Pole-star" (see Fig. 58). This star, though not one of the largest, is important, because it is very near that spot in the sky towards which the North Pole of our earth points. The consequence is, that though all the other stars appear to move in a circle round the heavens, and to be in different places at different seasons, this star remains always in the same place, only appearing to describe a very tiny circle in the sky round the exact spot to which our North Pole points.

Month after month and year after year it shines exactly over that thatched cottage yonder, which you see now immediately below it ; and wherever you are in the northern hemisphere, if you once note a certain tree, or chimney, or steeple which points upwards to the Pole-star, it will guide you to it at any hour on any night of the year, though the other constella-

tions will be now on one side, now on the other
side of it.

The Pole-star is really the front horse of a small
imitation of Charles's Wain, which, however, has never
been called by any special name, but only part of the
" Little Bear." Those two hind stars of the tiny
waggon, which are so much the brightest, are called
the " Guards," because they appear to move in a
circle round the Pole-star night after night and year
after year like sentries.

Opposite to them, on the farther side of the Pole-
star, is a well-marked constellation, a widespread W
written in the sky by five large stars ; the second V

Fig. 61.

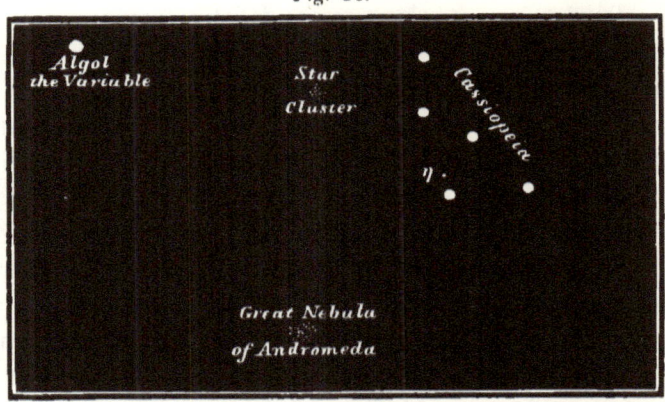

The constellation of Cassiopeia, and the heavenly bodies which
can be found by means of it.[1]

of the W has rather a longer point than the first, and
as we see it now the letter is almost upside down (see

---

[1] For Almach see Fig. 58, it has been accidentally omitted from
this figure.

Fig. 58). These are the five brightest stars in the constellation Cassiopeia, with a sixth not quite so bright in the third stroke of the W. You can never miss them when you have once seen them, even though they lie in the midst of a dense layer of the stars of the Milky Way, and if you have any difficulty at first, you have only to look as far on the one side of the Pole-star as the top hind star of Charles's Wain is on the other, and you must find them. I want to use them to-night chiefly as guides to find two remarkable objects which I hope you will look at again and again. The first is a small round misty patch not easy to see, but which you will find by following out the *second* stroke of the first V of the W. Beginning at the top, and following the line to the point of the V, continue on across the sky, and then search with your telescope till you catch a glimpse of this faint mist (*c*, Fig. 58 ; star-cluster, Fig. 61). You will see at once that it is sparkling all over with stars, for in fact you have actually before you in that tiny cluster more stars than you can see with the naked eye all over the heavens! Think for a moment what this means. One faint misty spot in the constellation Perseus, which we should have passed over unheeded without a telescope, proves to be a group of more than 3000 suns!

The second object you will find more easily, for it is larger and brighter, and appears as a faint dull spot to the naked eye. Going back to Cassiopeia, follow out the *second* V in the W from the top to the point of the V and onwards till your eye rests upon this misty cloud, which is called the Great Nebula of

Andromeda, and has sometimes been mistaken for a comet (Figs. 58 and 61). You will, however, be disappointed when you look through the telescope, for it will still only appear a mist, and you will be able to make nothing of it, except that instead of being of an irregular shape like Orion, it is elliptical ; and in a powerful telescope two dark rifts can be seen separating the streams of nebulous matter. These rifts are now shown in a photograph taken by Mr. Roberts, 1st October 1888, to be two vast dusky rings lying between the spiral stream of light, which winds in an ellipse till it ends in a small nucleus at the centre.

Ah ! you will say, this must be a cloud of gas like Orion's nebula, only winding round and round. No ! the spectroscope steps in here and tells us that the light shows something very much like a continuous spectrum, but not as long as it ought to be at the red end. Now, since gases give only bright lines, this nebula cannot be entirely gaseous. Then it must be made of stars too far off to see ? If so, it is very strange that though it is so dense and bright in some parts, and so spread out and clear in others, the most powerful telescopes cannot break it up into stars. In fact, the composition of the great nebula of Andromeda is still a mystery, and remains for one of you boys to study when he has become a great astronomer.

Still one more strange star we will notice before we leave this part of the heavens. You will find it, or at least go very near it, by continuing northwards the line you drew from Cassiopeia to the Star

Cluster (*c*, Fig. 58), and as it is a bright star, you will not miss it. That is to say, it is bright to-night and will remain so till to-morrow night, but if you come to me about nine o'clock to-morrow evening I will show you that it is growing dim, and if we had patience to watch through the night we should find, three or four hours later still, that it looks like one of the smaller stars. Then it will begin to brighten again, and in four hours more will be as bright as at first. It will remain so for nearly three days, or, to speak accurately, 2 days, 20 hours, 48 minutes, and 55 seconds, and then will begin to grow dull again. This star is called Algol the Variable. There are several such stars in the heavens, and we do not know why they vary, unless perhaps some dark globe passes round them, cutting off part of their light for a time.

And now, if your eyes are not weary, let us go back to the Pole-star and draw a line from it straight down the horizon due north. Shortly before we arrive there you will see a very brilliant bluish-white star a little to the east of this line. This is Vega, one of the brightest stars in the heavens except Sirius. It had not risen in the earlier part of the evening, but now it is well up and will appear to go on, steadily mounting as it circles round the Pole-star, till at four o'clock to-morrow morning it will be right overhead towards the south.

But beautiful as Vega is, a still more interesting star lies close to it (see Fig. 58). This small star, called ε Lyræ by astronomers, looks a little longer in one direction than in the other, and even with the naked eye some people can see a division in the middle dividing it into two stars. Your telescopes will show them

Fig. 62.

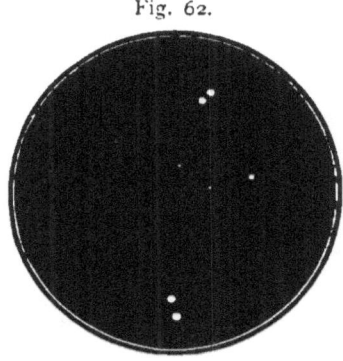

easily, and a powerful telescope tells a wonderful story, for it reveals that each of these two stars is again composed of two stars, so that ε Lyræ (Fig. 62) is really a double-double star. There is no doubt that each pair is a binary star, that is, the two stars move round each other very slowly, and possibly both pairs may also revolve round a common centre.

ε Lyræ. A double-binary star. Each couple revolves, and the couples probably also revolve round each other. (After Chambers.)

There are at least 10,000 double stars in the heavens; though, as we have seen, they are not all binary. The list of binary stars, however, increases every year as they are carefully examined, and probably about one star in three over the whole sky is made up of more than one sun.

Let us turn the telescope for a short time upon a few of the double stars and we shall have a great treat, for one of the most interesting facts about them is that both stars are rarely of the same colour. It seems strange at first to speak of stars as coloured, but they do not by any means all give out the same kind of light. Our sun is yellow, and so are the Pole-star and Pollux; but Sirius, Vega, and Regulus are dazzling

Plate II

COLOURED DOUBLE STARS.

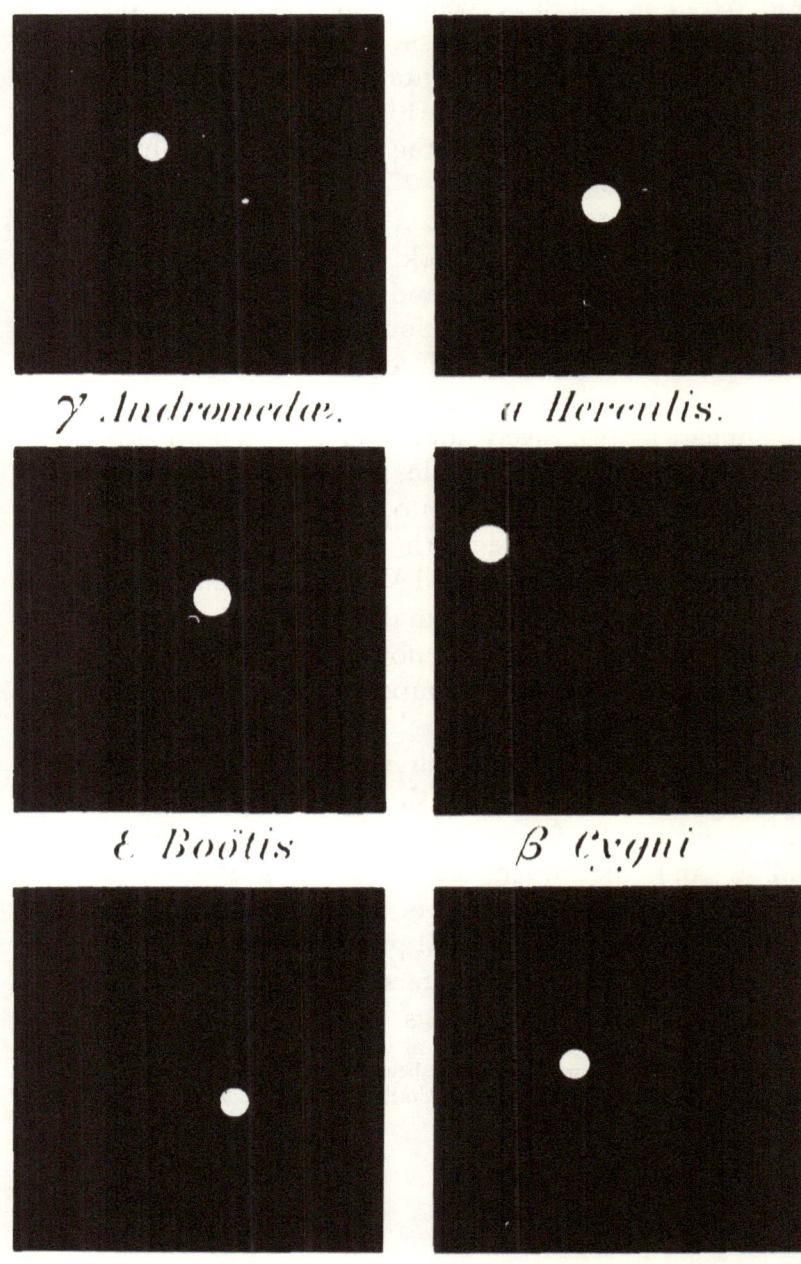

γ Andromedæ.

a Herculis.

ε Boötis

β Cygni

δ Geminorum

η Cassiopeiæ.

white or bluish-white, Arcturus is a yellowish-white, Aldebaran is a bright yellow-red, Betelgeux a deep orange-red, as you may see now in the telescope, for he is full in view ; while Antares, a star in the constellation of the Scorpion, which at this time of year cannot be seen till four in the morning, is an intense ruby red.

It appears to be almost a rule with double stars to be of two colours. Look up at Almach (γ Andromedæ), a bright star standing next to Algol the Variable in the sweep of four bright stars behind Cassiopeia (see Fig. 58). Even to the naked eye he appears to flash in a strange way, and in the telescope he appears as two lovely stars, one a deep orange and the other a pale green, while in powerful telescopes the green one splits again into two (Plate II.) Then again, η Cassiopeæ, the sixth star lying between the two large ones in the second V of Cassiopeia, divides into a yellow star and a small rich purple one, and δ Geminorum, a bright star not far from Pollux in the constellation Gemini, is composed of a large green star and a small purple one. Another very famous double star (β Cygni), which rises only a little later in the evening, lies below Vega a little to the left. It is composed of two lovely stars ; one an orange yellow and the other blue ; while ε Boötis, just visible above the horizon, is composed of a large yellow star and a very small green one.[1]

There are many other stars of two colours even among the few constellations we have picked out to-

[1] The plate of coloured stars has been most kindly drawn to scale and coloured for me by Mr. Arthur Cottam, F.R.A.S.

16

night, as, for example, the star at the top of the tail-
board of Charles's Waggon and the second horse Mizar.
Rigel in Orion, and the two outer stars of the belt,
a Herculis, which will rise later in the evening, and
the beautiful triple star (ζ Cancer) near the Beehive
(see Fig. 54), are all composed of two or more stars
of different colours.

Why do these suns give out such beautiful coloured
light?   The telescope cannot tell us, but the spectroscope again reveals the secrets so long hidden from
us.   By a series of very delicate experiments, Dr.
Huggins has shown that the light of all stars is sifted
before it comes to us, just as the light of our sun is ;
and those rays which are least cut off play most
strongly on our eyes, and give the colour to the star.
The question is a difficult one but I will try to give
you some idea of it, that you may form some picture
in your mind of what happens.

We learnt in our last lecture (p. 131) that the light
from our sun passes through the great atmosphere of
vapours surrounding him before it goes out into space,
and that many rays are in this way cut off ; so that
when we spread out his light in a long spectrum
there are dark lines or spaces where no light falls.[1]
Now in sunlight these dark lines are scattered pretty
evenly over the spectrum, so that about as much light
is cut off in one part as in another, and no one
colour is stronger than the rest.

Dr. Huggins found, however, that in coloured stars
the dark spaces are often crowded into particular
parts of the long band of colour forming the spectrum ;

[1] See No. 1 in Table of Spectra, Plate I.

showing that many of those light-rays have been cut off in the atmosphere round the star, and thus their particular colours are dimmed, leaving the other colour or colours more vivid. In red stars, for example, the yellow, blue, and green parts of the spectrum are much lined while the red end is strong and clear. With blue stars it is just the opposite, and the violet end is most free from dark lines. So there are really brilliantly coloured suns shining in the heavens, and in many cases two or more of these revolve round each other.

And now I have kept your attention and strained your eyes long enough, and you have objects to study for many a long evening before you will learn to see them plainly. You must not expect to find them every night, for the lightest cloud or the faintest moonlight will hide many of them from view; and, moreover, though you may learn to use the telescope fairly, you will often not know how to get a clear view with it. Still, you may learn a great deal, and before we go in I want to put a thought into your minds which will make astronomy still more interesting. We have seen that the stronger our telescopes the more stars, star-clusters, and nebulæ we see, and we cannot doubt that there are still countless heavenly bodies quite unknown to us. Some years ago Bessel the astronomer found that Sirius, in its real motion through the heavens, moves irregularly, travelling sometimes a little more slowly than at other times, and he suggested that some unseen companion must be pulling at him.

Twenty-eight years later, in 1862, two celebrated

opticians, father and son, both named Alvan Clark, were trying a new telescope at Chicago University, when suddenly the son, who was looking at Sirius, exclaimed, " Why, father, the star has a companion ! " And so it was. The powerful telescope showed what Bessel had foretold, and proved Sirius to be a " binary " star—that is, as we have seen, a star which has another moving round it.

It has since been proved that this companion is twenty-eight times farther from Sirius than we are from our sun, and moves round him in about forty-nine years. It is seven times as heavy as our sun, and yet gives out so little light that only the keenest telescopes can bring it into view.

Now if such a large body as this can give so very faint a light that we can scarcely see it, though Sirius, which is close to it, shines brightest of any star in the heavens, how many more bodies must there be which we shall never see, even among those which give out light, while how many there are dark like our earth, who can tell ?

Now that we know each of the stars to be a brilliant sun, many of them far, far brighter than ours, yet so like in their nature and laws, we can scarcely help speculating whether round these glorious suns, worlds of some kind may not be moving. If so, and there are people in them, what a strange effect those double coloured suns must produce with red daylight one day and blue daylight another !

Surely, as we look up at the myriads of stars bespangling the sky, and remember that our star-sun has seven planets moving round it of which one at least—our own earth—is full of living beings, we must picture these glorious suns as the centres of unseen systems, so that those twinkling specks become as suggestive as the faint lights of a great fleet far out at sea, which tell us of mighty ships, together with frigates and gunboats, full of living beings, though we cannot see them, nor even guess what they may be like. How insignificant we feel when we look upon that starlit sky and remember that the whole of our solar system would be but a tiny speck of light if seen as far off as we see the stars ! If our little earth and our short life upon it were all we could boast of we should be mites indeed.

But our very study to-night lifts us above these and reminds us that there is a spirit within us which even now can travel beyond the narrow bounds of our globe, measure the vast distances between us and the stars, gauge their brightness, estimate their weight, and discern their movements. As we gaze into the depths of the starlit sky, and travel onwards and onwards in imagination to those distant stars which photography alone reveals to us, do not our hearts leap at the thought of a day which must surely come when, fettered and bound no longer to earth, this spirit shall wander forth and penetrate some of the mystery of those mighty suns at which we now gaze in silent awe.

CHAPTER VIII

LITTLE BEINGS FROM A MINIATURE OCEAN

IN our last lecture we soared far away into boundless space, and lost ourselves for a time among seen and unseen suns. In this lecture we will come back not merely to our little world, nor even to one of the widespread oceans which cover so much of it, but to one single pool lying just above the limits of low tide, so that it is only uncovered for a very short time every day. This pool is to be found in a secluded bay within an hour's journey by train from this college, and only a few miles from Torquay. It has no name, so far as I know, nor do many people visit it, otherwise I should not have kept my little pool so long undisturbed. As it is, however, for many years past I have had only to make sure as to the time of low tide, and put myself in the train ; and then, unless the sea was very rough and stormy, I could examine the little inhabitants of my miniature ocean in peace.

The pool lies in a deep hollow among a group of rocks and boulders, close to the entrance of the cove, which can only be entered at low water ; it does not measure more than two feet across, so that you can step over it, if you take care not to slip on the masses of green and brown seaweed growing over the rocks on its sides, as I have done many a time when collecting specimens for our salt-water aquarium. I find now the only way is to lie flat down on the rock, so that my hands and eyes are free to observe and handle, and then, bringing my eye down to the edge of the pool, to lift the seaweeds and let the sunlight enter into the chinks and crannies. In this way I can catch sight of many a small being either on the seaweed or the rocky ledges, and even creatures transparent as glass become visible by the thin out-line gleaming in the sunlight. Then I pluck a piece of seaweed, or chip off a fragment of rock with a sharp-edged collecting knife, bringing away the speci-men uninjured upon it, and place it carefully in its own separate bottle to be carried home alive and well.

Now though this little pool and I are old friends, I find new treasures in it almost every time I go, for it is almost as full of living things as the heavens are of stars, and the tide as it comes and goes brings many a mother there to find a safe home for her little ones, and many a waif and stray to seek shelter from the troublous life of the open ocean.

You will perhaps find it difficult to believe that

in this rock-bound basin there can be millions of living creatures hidden away among the fine feathery weeds ; yet so it is. Not that they are always the same. At one time it may be the home of myriads of infant crabs, not an eighth of an inch long, at another of baby sea-urchins only visible to the naked eye as minute spots in the water, at another of young jelly-fish growing on their tiny stalks, and splitting off one by one as transparent bells to float away with the rising tide. Or it may be that the whelk has chosen this quiet nook to deposit her leathery eggs ; or young barnacles, periwinkles, and limpets are growing up among the green and brown tangles, while the far-sailing velella and the stay-at-home sea-squirts, together with a variety of other sea-animals, find a nursery and shelter in their youth in this quiet harbour of rest.

And besides these casual visitors there are numberless creatures which have lived and multiplied there, ever since I first visited the pool. Tender red, olive-coloured, and green seaweeds, stony corallines, and acorn-barnacles lining the floor, sea-anemones clinging to the sides, sponges tiny and many-coloured hiding under the ledges, and limpets and mussels wedged in the cracks. These can be easily seen with the naked eye, but they are not the most numerous inhabitants ; for these we must search with a magnifying-glass, which will reveal to us wonderful fairy-forms, delicate crystal vases with tiny creatures in them whose transparent lashes make whirlpools in the water, living crystal bells so tiny that whole branches of them look only like a fringe of hair, jelly globes rising and falling in the water, patches of living jelly clinging to the rocky sides of the pool, and a hundred other forms, some so minute that you must examine the fine sand in which they lie under a powerful microscope before you can even guess that they are there.

So it has proved a rich hunting-ground, where summer and winter, spring and autumn, I find some form to put under my magic glass. There I can watch it for weeks growing and multiplying under my care ; moved only from the aquarium, where I keep it supplied with healthy sea-water, to the tiny transparent trough in which I place it for a few

Fig. 63.

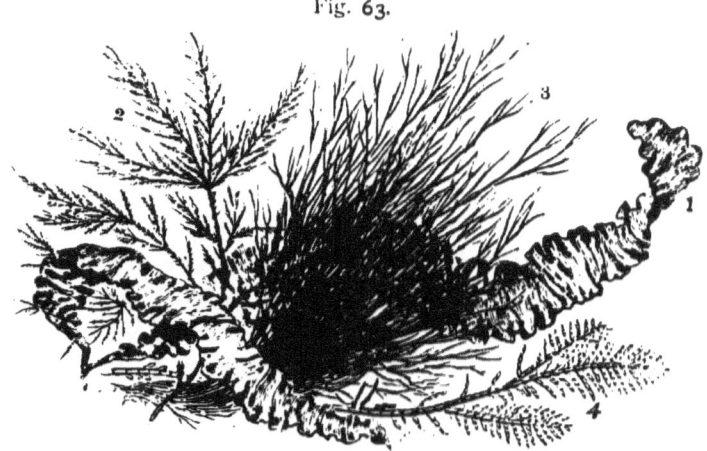

Group of seaweeds (natural size).

1, *Ulva Linza.*   2, *Sphacelaria filicina.*   3, *Polysiphonia urceolata.*
4, *Corallina officinalis.*

hours to see the changes it has undergone. I could tell you endless tales of transformations in these tiny lives, but I want to-day to show you a few of my friends, most of which I brought yesterday fresh from the pool, and have prepared for you to examine.

Let us begin with seaweeds. I have said that there are three leading colours in my pool—green, olive, and red—and these tints mark roughly three kinds of weed, though they occur in an endless variety of shapes. Here is a piece of the beautiful pale green seaweed, called the Laver or Sea-lettuce, *Ulva Linza* (1, Fig. 63), which grows in long ribbons in a sunny nook in the water. I have placed under the first microscope a piece of this weed which is just sending out young seaweeds in the shape of tiny cells, with lashes very like those we saw coming from the moss-flower, and I have pressed them in the position in which they would naturally leave the plant (*ss*, Fig. 64.).[1] You will also see on this slide several cells in which these tiny spores *s* are forming, ready to burst out and swim ; for this green weed is merely a collection of cells,

Fig. 64.

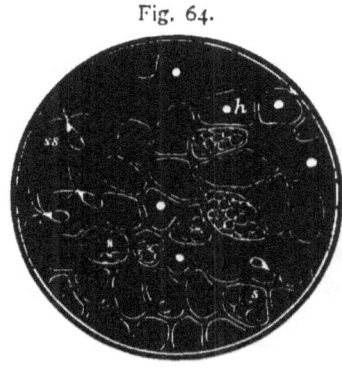

Ulva lactuca, a green seaweed, greatly magnified to show structure. (After Oersted.)

s, Spores in the cells. *ss*, Spores swimming out. *h*, Holes through which spores have escaped.

[1] The slice given in Fig. 64 is from a broader-leaved form, *U. lactuca*, because this species, being composed of only one layer of cells, is better seen. *Ulva linza* is composed of two layers of cells.

like the single-celled plants on land. Each cell can work as a separate plant; it feeds, grows, and can send out its own young spores.

This deep olive-green feathery weed (2, Fig. 63), of which a piece is magnified under the next microscope (2, Fig. 65), is very different. It is a higher plant, and works harder for its living, using the darker rays of sunlight which penetrate into shady parts of the pool. So it comes to pass that its cells divide the work. Those of the feathery threads make the food, while others, growing on short stalks on the shafts of the feather make and send out the young spores.

Lastly, the lovely red threadlike weeds, such as this *Polysiphonia urceolata* (3, Fig. 63), carry actual urns on their stems like those of mosses. In fact, the history of these urns (see No. 3, Fig. 65) is much the same in the two classes of plants, only that instead of the urn being pushed up on a thin stalk as in the moss, it re-

Fig. 65.

Three seaweeds of Fig. 63 much magnified to show fruits. (Harvey.)

2, *Sphacelaria filicina.* 3, *Polysiphonia urceolata.* 4, *Corallina officinalis.*

mains on the seaweed close down to the stem, when it grows out of the plant-egg, and the tiny plant is shut in till the spores are ready to swim out.

The stony corallines (4, Figs. 63 and 65), which build so much carbonate of lime into their stems, are near relations of the red seaweeds. There are plenty of them in my pool. Some of them, of a deep purple colour, grow upright in stiff groups about three or four inches high; and others, which form crusts over the stones and weeds, are a pale rose colour; but both kinds, when the plant dies, leaving the stony skeleton (1, Fig. 66), are a pure white, and used to be mistaken for corals. They belong to the same order of plants as the red weeds, which all live in shady nooks in the pools, and are the highest of their race.

My pool is full of different forms of these four weeds. The green ribbons float on the surface rooted to the sides of the pool and, as the sun shines upon it, the glittering bubbles rising from them show that they are working up food out of the air in the water, and giving off oxygen. The brown weeds lie chiefly under the shelves of rocks, for they can manage with less sunlight, and use the darker rays which pass by the green weeds; and last of all, the red weeds and corallines, small and delicate in form, line the bottom of the pool in its darkest nooks.

And now if I hand round two specimens—one a coralline, and the other something you do not yet know—I am sure you will say at first sight that they belong to the same family, and, in fact, if you buy at the seaside a group of seaweeds gummed on paper, you will most likely get both these among them. Yet the truth is, that while the coralline (1, Fig. 66) is a plant, the other specimen (2) which is called *Sertularia filicula*, is an animal.

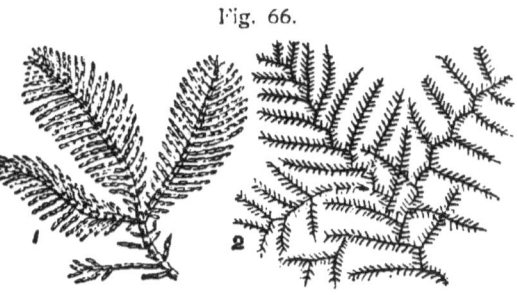

Fig. 66.

This special sertularian grows upright in my pool on stones or often on seaweeds, but I have here (Fig. 67)

Coralline and Sertularia, to show likeness between the animal Sertularia and the plant Coralline.

1, *Corallina officinalis*. 2, *Sertularia filicula*.

another and much smaller one which lives literally in millions hanging its cups downwards. I find it not only under the narrow ledges of the pool sheltered by the seaweed, but forming a fringe along all the rocks on each side of the cove near to low-water mark, and for a long time I passed it by thinking it was of no interest. But I have long since given up thinking this of anything, especially in my pool, for my magic glass has taught me that there is not even a living speck which does not open out into something marvellous and beautiful. So I chipped off a small piece of rock and brought the fringe home, and found, when I hung it up in clear sea water as I have done over this glass trough (Fig. 67) and looked at it through the lens, that each thread of the dense fringe, in itself not a quarter of an inch deep, turns out to be a tiny sertularian with at least twenty mouths. You can see this with your pocket

17

lens even as it hangs here, and when you have
examined it you can by and by take off one thread
and put it carefully
in the trough.   I
promise you a sight
of the most beautiful
little beings which
exist in nature.

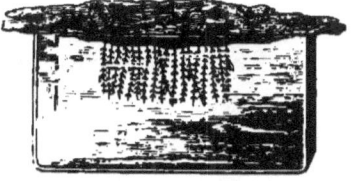

Fig. 67.

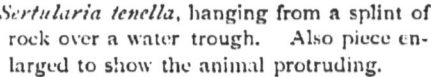

Sertularia tenella, hanging from a splint of
rock over a water trough.   Also piece enlarged to show the animal protruding.

Come and look at
it after the lecture.
It   is   a   horny
branched stem with
a double row of tiny cups all along each side
(see Fig. 67).   Out of these cups there appear
from time to time sixteen minute transparent tentacles as fine as spun glass, which wave about
in the water.   If you shake the glass a little, in
an instant each crystal star vanishes into its cup,
to come out again a few minutes later ; so that now
here, now there, the delicate animal-flowers spread
out on each side of the stem, and the tree is covered
with moving beings.   These tentacles are feelers,
which lash food into a mouth and stomach in each
cup, where it is digested and passed, through a hole
in the bottom, along a jelly thread which runs down
the stem and joins all the mouths together.   In this
way the food is distributed all over the tree, which is,
in fact, one animal with many feeding-cups.   Some
day I will show you one of these cups with the
tentacles stretched out and mounted on a slide, so
that you can examine a tentacle with a very strong
magnifying power.   You will then see that it is

dotted over with cells, in which are coiled fine threads. The animal uses these threads to paralyse the creatures on which it feeds, for at the base of each thread there is a poison gland.

In the larger Sertularia (2, Fig. 66) the whole branched tree is connected by jelly threads running through the stem, and all the thousands of mouths are spread out in the water. One large form called the sea-fir *Sertularia cupressina* grows sometimes three feet high, and bears as many as a hundred thousand cups, with living mouths, on its branches.

The next of my minute friends I can only show to the class in a diagram, but you will see it under the fourth microscope by and by. I had great trouble in finding it yesterday, though I knew its haunts upon the green weed, for it is so minute and trans-parent that even when the weed is in a trough a magnifying-glass will scarcely detect it. And I must warn you that if you want to know any of the minute creatures we are studying, you must visit one place constantly. You may in a casual way find many of them on seaweed, or in the damp ooze and mud, but it will be by chance only ; to look for them with any certainty you must take trouble in making their acquaintance.

Turning then to the diagram (Fig. 68) I will describe it as I hope you will see it under the microscope—a curious tiny, perfectly transparent open-mouthed vase standing upright on the weed, and having an equally transparent being rising up in it and waving its tiny lashes in the water. This is really all one animal, the vase *hc* being the horny covering or carapace of the body, which last stands up like a tube in the centre. If you watch carefully,

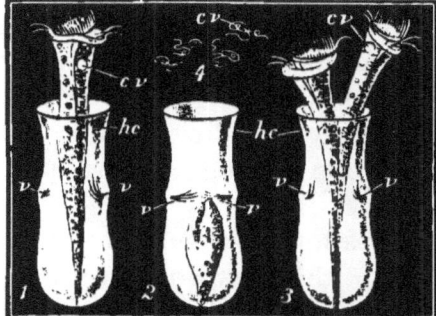

Fig. 68.

Thuricolla folliculata and *Chilomonas amygdalum.* (Saville Kent.)

1, Thuricolla erect ; 2, retracted ; 3, dividing. 4, *Chilomonas amygdalum. hc,* Horny carapace. *cv,* Contractile vesicle. *v,* Closing valves.

you may even see the minute atoms of food twisting round inside the tube until they are digested, after they have been swept in at the wide open mouth by the whirling lashes. You will see this more clearly if you put a little rice-flour, very minutely powdered and coloured by carmine, into the water ; for you can trace these red atoms into some round spaces called *vacuoles* which are dotted over the body of the animal, and are really globules of watery fluid in which the food is probably partly digested.

You will notice, however, one round clear space (*cv*) into which they do not go, and after a time you will be able to observe that this round spot closes up or contracts very quickly, and then expands again very slowly. As it expands it fills with a clear fluid, and naturalists have not yet decided exactly what work it does. It may serve the animal either for breathing, or as a very simple heart, making the fluids circulate in the tube. The next interesting point about this little being is the way it retreats into its sheltering vase. Even while you are watching, it is quite likely it may all at once draw itself down to the bottom as in No. 2, and folding down the valves *v*, *v* of horny teeth which grow on each side, shut itself in from some fancied danger. Another very curious point is that, besides sending forth young ones, these creatures multiply by dividing in two (see No. 3, Fig. 68), each one closing its own part of the vase into a new home.

There are hundreds of these *Infusoria*, as they are called, in my pond, some with vases, some without, some fixed to weeds and stones, others swimming about freely. Even in the water-trough in which this Thuricolla stands, I saw several smaller forms, and the next microscope has a trough filled with the minutest form of all, called a Monad (No. 4, Fig. 68). These are so small that 2000 of them would lie side by side in an inch; that is, if you could make them lie at all, for they are the most restless little beings, darting hither and thither, scarcely even halting except to turn back. And yet though there are so many of them, and as far as we know they have no organs of sight, they never run up against each other, but glide past more cleverly than any clear-sighted fish. These creatures are mostly to be found among decaying seaweed, and though they are so tiny, you can still see distinctly the clear space (*cv*) contracting and expanding within them.

But if there are so many thousands of mouths to feed, on the tree-like *Sertulariæ* as well as in all these *Infusoria*, where does the food come from?

Partly from the numerous atoms of decaying life all around, and the minute eggs of animals and spores of plants ; but besides these, the pool is full of minute living plants—small jelly masses with solid coats of flint which are moulded into most lovely shapes.   Plants formed of jelly and flint !   You will think I am joking, but I am not.   These plants, called *Diatoms*, which live both in salt and fresh water, are single cells feeding and growing just like those we took from the water-butt (Fig. 29, p. 78), only that instead of a soft covering they build up a flinty skeleton.

Fig. 69.

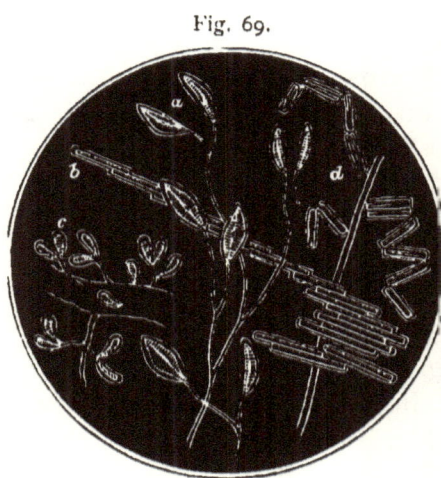

Living diatoms.

a, Cocconema lanceolatum.   b, Bacillaria paradoxa.   c, Gomphonema marinum.   d, Diatoma hyalina.

They are so small, that many of them must be magnified to fifty times their real size before you can even see them distinctly.   Yet the skeletons of these almost invisible plants are carved and chiselled in the most delicate patterns.   I showed you a group of these in our lecture on magic glasses (p. 39), and now I have brought a few living ones that we may learn to know them.   The diagram (Fig. 69) shows the chief forms you will see on the different slides.

The first one, *Bacillaria paradoxa* (*b*, Fig. 69), looks like a number of rods clinging one to another in a string, but each one of these is a single-celled plant with a jelly cell surrounding the flinty skeleton. You will see that they move to and fro over each other in the water.

The next two forms, *a* and *c*, look much more like plants, for the cells arrange themselves on a jelly stem, which by and by disappears, leaving only the separate flint skeletons such as you see in Fig. 16. The last form, *d*, is something midway between the other forms, the separate cells hang on to each other and also on to a straight jelly stem.

Another species of Diatoma (Fig. 70) called *Diatoma vulgare*, is a very simple and common form, and will help to explain how these plants grow. The

Fig. 70.

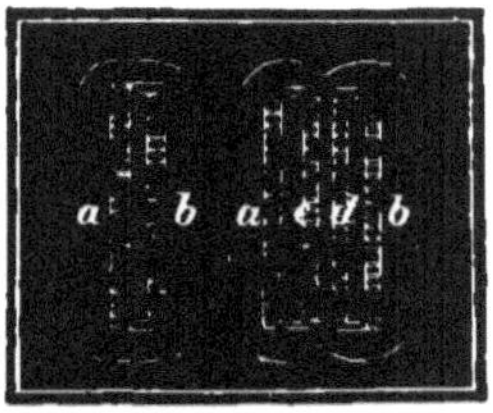

A diatom (*Diatoma vulgare*) growing.

a, *b*, Flint skeleton inside the jelly-cell. *a*, *c* and *d*, *b*, Two flint skeletons formed by new valves, *c* and *d*, forming within the first skeleton.

two flinty valves *a*, *b* inside the cell are not quite the same size ; the older one *a* is larger than the younger one *b* and fits over it like the cover of a pill-box. As the plant grows, the cell enlarges and forms two more valves, one *c* fitting into the cover *a*, so as to make a complete box *ac*, and a second, *d*, back to back with *c*, fitting into the valve *b*, and making another complete box *bd*. This goes on very rapidly, and in this plant each new cell separates as it is formed, and the free diatoms move about quite actively in the water.

If you consider for a moment, you will see that, as the new valves always fit into the old ones, each must be smaller than the last, and so there comes a time when the valves have become too small to go on increasing. Then the plant must begin afresh. So the two halves of the last cell open, and throwing out their flinty skeletons, cover themselves with a thin jelly layer, and form a new cell which grows larger than any of the old ones. These, which are spore-cells, then form flinty valves inside, and the whole thing begins again.

Now though the plants themselves die, or become the food of minute animals, the flinty skeletons are not destroyed, but go on accumulating in the waters of ponds, lakes, rivers, and seas, all over the world. Untold millions have no doubt crumbled to dust and gone back into the waters, but untold millions also have survived. The towns of Berlin in Europe and of Richmond in the United States are actually built upon ground called "infusorial earth," composed almost entirely of valves of these minute diatoms which have accumulated to a thickness of more than eighty feet! Those under Berlin are fresh-water forms, and must have lived in a lake, while those of Richmond belong to salt-water forms. Every inch of the ground under those cities represents thousands and thousands of living plants which flourished in ages long gone by, and were no larger than those you will see presently under the microscope.

These are a very few of the microscopic inhabitants of my pond, but, as you will confuse them if I show you too many, we will conclude with two rather larger specimens, and examine them carefully. The first, called the Cydippe, is a lovely, transparent living ball, which I want to explain to you because it is so wondrously beautiful. The second, the Sea-mat or Flustra, looks like a crumpled drab-coloured seaweed,

Fig. 71.

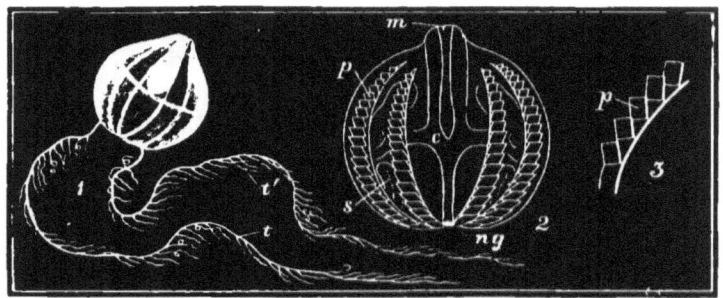

Cydippe Pileus.

1, Animal with tentacles *t*, bearing small tendrils *t'*. 2, Body of animal enlarged. *m*, Mouth. *c*, Digestive cavity. *s*, Sac into which the tentacles are withdrawn. *p*, Bands with comb-like plates. 3, Portion of a band enlarged to show the moving plates *p*.

but is really composed of many thousands of grottos, the homes of tiny sea-animals.

Let us take the Cydippe first (1, Fig. 71). I have six here, each in a separate tumbler, and could have brought many more, for when I dipped my net in the pool yesterday such numbers were caught in it that I believe the retreating tide must just have left a shoal behind. Put a tumbler on the desk in front of you, and if the light falls well upon it you will see a transparent ball about the size of a large pea marked with eight bright bands, which begin at the lower end of the ball and reach nearly to the top, dividing the outside into sections like the ribs of a melon. The creature is so perfectly transparent that you can count all the eight bands.

At the top of the ball is a slight bulge which is the mouth (*m* 2, Fig. 71), and from it, inside the ball, hangs a long bag or stomach, which opens below into a cavity *c*, from which two canals branch out, one on each side, and these divide again into four canals which go one into each of the tubes running down the bands. From this cavity the food, which is digested in the stomach, is carried by the canals all over the body. The smaller tubes which branch out of these canals cannot be seen clearly without a very strong lens, and the only other parts you can discern in this transparent ball are two long sacs on each side of the lower end. These are the tentacle sacs, in which are coiled up the tentacles, which we shall describe presently. Lastly, you can notice that the bands outside the globe are broader in the middle than at the ends, and are striped across by a number of ridges.

In moving the tumblers the water has naturally been shaken, and the creature being alarmed will probably at first remain motionless. But very soon it will begin to play in the water, rising and falling, and swimming gracefully from side to side. Now you will notice a curious effect, for the bands will glitter and become tinged with prismatic colours, till, as it moves more and more rapidly these colours, reflected in the jelly, seem to tinge the whole ball with colours like those on a soap-bubble, while from the two sacs below come forth two long transparent threads like spun glass.   At first these appear to be simple threads, but as they gradually open out to about four or five inches, smaller threads uncoil on each side of the line till there are about fifty on each line.   These short *tendrils* are never still for long ; as the main threads wave to and fro, some of the shorter ones coil up and hang like tiny beads, then these uncoil and others roll up, so that these graceful floating lines are never two seconds alike.

We do not really know their use.   Sometimes the creature anchors itself by them, rising and falling as they stretch out or coil up ; but more often they float idly behind it in the water.   At first you would perhaps think that they served to drive the ball through the water, but this is done by a special apparatus.   The cross ridges which we noticed on the bands are really flat comb-like plates (*p*, Fig. 71), of which there are about twenty or thirty on each band ; and these vibrate very rapidly, so that two hundred or more paddles drive the tiny ball through the water.   This is the cause of the prismatic colours ; for iridescent tints are produced by the play of light upon the glittering plates, as they incessantly change their angle.   Sometimes they move all at once, sometimes only a few at a time, and it is evident the creature controls them at will.

This lovely fairy-like globe, with its long floating tentacles and rainbow tints, was for a long time classed with the jelly-fish ; but it really is most nearly

related to sea-anemones, as it has a true central
cavity which acts as a stomach, and many other
points in common with the *Actinozoa*.   We cannot
help wondering, as the little being glides hither and
thither, whether it can see where it is going.   It has
nerves of a low kind which start from a little dark
spot (*ng*), exactly at the south pole of the ball, and
at that point a sense-organ of some kind exists, but
what impression the creature gains from it of the
world outside we cannot tell.

I am afraid you may think it dull to turn from
such a beautiful being as this, to the grey leaf which
looks only like a dead dry seaweed ; yet you will be
wrong, for a more wonderful history attaches to this
crumpled dead-looking leaf than to the lovely jelly-
globe.

First of all I will pass round pieces of the dry leaf
(1, Fig. 72), and while you are getting them I will tell
you where I found the living ones.   Great masses of
the Flustra, as it is called, line the bottom and sides
of my pool.   They grow in tufts, standing upright
on the rock, and looking exactly like hard grey
seaweeds, while there is nothing to lead you to
suspect that they are anything else.   Yesterday I
chipped off very carefully a piece of rock with a tuft
upon it, and have kept it since in a glass globe by
itself with sea-water, for the little creatures living in
this marine city require a very good supply of healthy
water and air.   I have called it a " marine city," and
now I will tell you why.   Take the piece in your
hand and run your finger gently up and down it ;
you will glide quite comfortably from the lower to

the higher part of the leaf, but when you come back
you will feel your finger catch slightly on a rough
surface. Your pocket lens will show why this is,
for if you look
through it at the
surface of the leaf
you will see it is
not smooth, but
composed of hun-
dreds of tiny al-
coves with arched
tops ; and on each
side of these tops
stand two short
blunt spines (see
2, Fig. 72), making

Fig. 72.

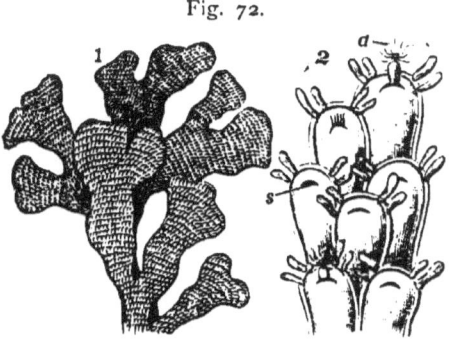

The Sea-mat or Flustra (*Flustra foliacea.*)
1, Natural size.   2, Much magnified.
s, Slit caused by drawing in of the animal *a*.

four in all, pointing upwards, so as partly to cover
the alcove above. As your finger went up it glided
over the spines, but on coming back it met their
points. This is all you can see in the dead specimen ;
I must show you the rest by diagrams, and by and
by under the microscope.

First, then, in the living specimen which I have here,
those alcoves are not open as in the dead piece, but
covered over with a transparent skin, in which, near
the top of the alcove just where the curve begins, is
a slit (*s* 2, Fig. 72). Unfortunately the membrane
covering this alcove is too dense for you to distinguish
the parts within. Presently, however, if you are
watching a piece of this living leaf in a flat water-
cell under the microscope, you will see the slit slowly
open, and begin to turn as it were inside out, exactly

18

like the finger of a glove, which has been pushed in at the tip, gradually rises up when you put your finger inside it.   As this goes on, a bundle of threads appears, at first closed like a bud, but gradually opening out into a crown of tentacles (*a*, Fig. 72), each one clothed with hairs.   Then you will see that the slit was not exactly a slit after all, but the round edge where the sac was pushed in.   Ah ! you will say, you are now showing me a polyp like those on the sertularian tree.   Not so fast, my friend ; you have not yet studied what is still under the covering skin and hidden in the living animal.   I have, however, prepared a slide with this membrane removed (see Fig. 73), and there you can observe the different parts, and learn that each one of these alcoves contains a complete animal, and not merely one among many mouths, like the polyp on the Sertularia.

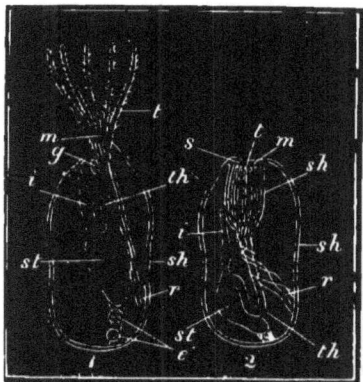

Fig. 73.

Diagram of the animal in the Flustra or Sea-mat.

1, Animal protruding. 2, Animal retracted in the sheath. *sh*, Covering sheath. *s*, Slit. *t*, Tentacles. *m*, Mouth. *th*, Throat. *st*, Stomach. *i*, Intestine. *r*, Retractor muscle. *e*, Egg - forming parts. *g*, Nerve-ganglion.

Each of these little beings (*a*, Fig 72) living in its alcove has a mouth, throat, stomach, intestine, muscles, and nerves starting from the ganglion of nervous matter, besides all that is necessary for producing eggs and sending forth young ones. You can trace all these under the microscope (see 2, Fig. 73) as the creature lies curiously doubled up in its bed, with its body bent in a loop; the intestine *i*, out of which the refuse food passes, coming back close up to the slit. When it is at rest, the top of the sac in which it lies is pulled in by the retractor muscle *r*, and looks, as I have said, like the finger of a glove with the top pushed in. When it wishes to feed, this top is drawn out by muscles running round the sac, and the tentacles open and wave in the water (1, Fig. 73).

Look now at the alcoves, the homes of these animals; see how tiny they are and how closely they fit together. Mr. Gosse, the naturalist, has reckoned that there are 6720 alcoves in a square inch; then if you turn the leaf over you will see that there is another set, fixed back to back with these, on the other side, making in all 13,440 alcoves. Now a moderate-sized leaf of flustra measures about three square inches, taking all the rounded lobes into account, so you will see we get 40,320 as a rough estimate of the number of beings on this one leaf. But if you look at this tuft I have brought, you will find it is composed of twelve such leaves, and this after all is a very small part of the mass growing round my pool. Was I wrong, then, when I said that my miniature ocean contains as many millions of beings as there are stars in the heavens?

You will want to know how these leaves grew, and it is in this way. First a little free swimming animal, a mere living sac provided with lashes, settles down and grows into one little horny alcove, with its live creature inside, which in time sends off from it three to five buds, forming alcoves all round the top and sides of the first one, growing on to it. These again bud out, and you can thus easily understand that, in this way, in time a good-sized leaf is formed. Meanwhile the creatures also send forth new swimming cells, which settle down near to begin new leaves, and thus a tuft is formed ; and long after the beings in earlier parts of the leaf have died and left their alcoves empty, those round the margin are still alive and spreading.

With this history we must stop for to-day, and I expect it will be many weeks before you have thoroughly examined the specimens of each kind which I have put in the aquarium. If you can trace the spore-cells and urns in the seaweeds, observe the polyps in the Sertularia, and count the number of mouths on a branch of my animal fringe (*Sertularia tenella*); if you make acquaintance with the Thuricolla in its vase, and are fortunate enough to see one divide in two ; if you learn to know some of the beautiful forms of diatoms, and can picture to yourselves the life of the tiny inhabitants of the Flustra ; then you will have used your microscope with some effect, and be prepared for an expedition to my pool, where we will go together some day to seek new treasures.

CHAPTER IX

THE DARTMOOR PONIES,

OR

THE WANDERINGS OF THE HORSE TRIBE

PUT away the telescopes and microscopes to-day, boys, the holidays are close at hand, and we will take a rest from peep-ing and peering till we come back in the autumn laden with specimens for the micro-scope, while the rapidly darken-ing evenings will tempt us again on to the lawn star-gazing. On this our last lecture-day I want you to take a journey with me which I took in imagina-tion a few days ago, as I lay on my back on the sunny moor and watched the Dartmoor ponies.

It was a calm misty morning one day last week, giving promise of a bright and sunny day, when I started off for a long walk across the moor to visit the famous stone-circles, many of which are to be found not far off the track, called Abbot's Way, leading from Buckfast Abbey, on the Dart, to the Abbey of Tavistock, on the Tavy.

My mind was full of the olden times as I pictured to myself how, seven hundred years or more ago, some Benedictine monk from Tavistock Abbey, in his black robe and cowl, paced this narrow path on his way to his Cistercian brethren at Buckfast, meeting some of them on his road as they wandered over the desolate moor in their white robes and black scapularies in search of stray sheep. For the Cistercians were shepherds and wool-weavers, while the Benedictines devoted themselves to learning, and the track of about twenty-five miles from one abbey to the other, which still remains, was worn by the members of the two communities and their dependents, the only variety in whose lives consisted probably in these occasional visits one to the other.

Yet even these monks belonged to modern times compared to the ancient Britons who raised the stone-circles, and buried their dead in the barrows scattered here and there over the moor ; and my mind drifted back to the days when, long before that pathway was worn, men clad in the skins of beasts hunted wild animals over the ground on which I was treading, and lived in caves and holes of the ground.

I wondered, as I thought of them, whether the cultured monks and the uncivilised Britons delighted as much in the rugged scenery of the moor as I did that morning. For many miles in front of me the moor stretched out wild and treeless ; the sun was

shining brightly upon the mass of yellow furze and
deep-red heather, drawing up the moisture from the
ground, and causing a kind of watery haze to shim-
mer over the landscape ; while the early mist was
rising off the *tors*, or hill-tops, in the distance,
curling in fanciful wreaths around the rugged and
stony summits, as it dispersed gradually in the
increasing heat of the day.

The cattle which were scattered in groups here
and there feeding on the dewy grass were enjoying
the happiest time of the year. The moor, which in
winter affords them scarcely a bare subsistence, is
now richly covered with fresh young grass, and the
sturdy oxen fed solemnly and deliberately, while the
wild Dartmoor ponies and their colts scampered
joyously along, shaking their manes and long flowing
tails, and neighing to each other as they went ; or
clustered together on some verdant spot, where the
colts teased and bit each other for fun, as they gam-
bolled round their mothers.

It was a pleasure, there on the open moor, with
the lark soaring overhead, and the butterflies and
bees hovering among the sweet-smelling furze blossoms, to see horses free and joyous, with no thought
of bit or bridle, harness or saddle, whose hoofs had
never been handled by the shoeing-smith, nor their
coats touched with the singeing iron. Those little
colts, with their thick heads, shaggy coats, and flowing tails, will have at least two years more freedom
before they know what it is to be driven or beaten.
Only once a year are they gathered together, claimed
by their owners and branded with an initial, and then

left again to wander where they will. True, it is a freedom which sometimes has its drawbacks, for if the winter is severe the only food they can get will be the furze-tops, off which they scrape the snow with their feet ; yet it is very precious in itself, for they can gallop when and where they choose, with head erect, sniffing at the wind and crying to each other for the very joy of life.

Now as I strolled across the moor and watched their gambols, thinking how like free wild animals they seemed, my thoughts roamed far away, and I saw in imagination scenes where other untamed animals of the horse tribe are living unfettered all their lives long.

First there rose before my mind the level grass-covered pampas of South America, where wild horses share the boundless plains with troops of the rhea, or American ostrich, and wander, each horse with as many mares as he can collect, in companies of hundreds or even thousands in a troop. These horses are now truly wild, and live freely from youth to age, unless they are unfortunate enough to be caught in the more inhabited regions by the lasso of the hunter. In the broad pampas, the home of herds of wild cattle, they dread nothing. There, as they roam with one bold stallion as their leader, even beasts of prey hesitate to approach them, for, when they form into a dense mass with the mothers and young in their centre, their heels deal blows which even the fierce jaguar does not care to encounter, and they trample their enemy to death in a very short time. Yet these are not the original wild horses we are seeking, they are the descendants of tame animals, brought from Europe by the Spaniards to Buenos Ayres in 1535, whose descendants have regained their freedom on the boundless pampas and prairies.

As I was picturing them careering over the plains, another scene presented itself and took their place. Now I no longer saw around me tall pampas-grass with the long necks of the rheas appearing above it, for I was on the edge of a dreary scantily covered plain between the Aral Sea and the Balkash Lake in Tartary. To the south lies a barren sandy desert, to the north the fertile plains of the Kirghiz steppes, where the Tartar feeds his flocks, and herds of antelopes gallop over the fresh green pasture ; and between these is a kind of no-man's land, where low scanty shrubs and stunted grass seemed to promise but a poor feeding-ground.

Yet here the small long-legged but powerful " Tarpans," the wild horses of the treeless plains of Russia and Tartary, were picking their morning meal. Sturdy wicked little fellows they are, with their shaggy light-brown coats, short wiry manes, erect ears, and fiery watchful eyes. They might well be supposed to be true wild horses, whose ancestors had never been tamed by man ; and yet it is more probable that even they escaped in early times from the Tartars, and have held their own ever since, over the grassy steppes of Russia and on the confines of the plains of Tartary. Sometimes they live almost alone, especially on the barren wastes where they have been seen in winter, scraping the snow off the herbage as our ponies do on Dartmoor. At other times, as in the south of Russia, where they wander between the Dnieper and the Don, they gather in vast herds and live a free life, not fearing even the wolves, which they beat to the ground with their hoofs. From one green oasis to another they travel over miles of ground.

> " A thousand horse—and none to ride !
> With flowing tail, and flying mane,
> Wide nostrils—never stretch'd by pain,
> Mouths bloodless to the bit or rein,
> And feet that iron never shod,
> And flanks unscarr'd by spur or rod.
> A thousand horse, the wild, the free,
> Like waves that follow o'er the sea." [1]

As I followed them in their course I fancied I saw troops of yet another animal of the horse tribe, the " Kulan," or *Equus hemionus,* which is a kind of half horse, half ass (Fig. 74), living on the Kirghiz steppes of Tartary and spreading far beyond the range of the Tarpan into Tibet. Here at last we have a truly wild animal, never probably brought into subjection by man. The number of names he possesses shows how widely he has spread. The Tartars call him " Kulan," the Tibetans " Kiang," while the Mongolians give him the unpronounceable name of " Dschiggetai." He will not submit to any of them, but if caught and confined soon breaks away again to his old life, a " free and fetterless creature."

No one has ever yet settled the question whether he is a horse or an ass, probably because he repre-

[1] Byron's *Mazeppa.*

sents an animal truly between the two. His head
is graceful, his body light, his legs slender and fleet,
yet his ears are long and ass-like; he has narrow
hoofs, and a tail with a tuft at the end like all the
ass tribe; his colour is a yellow brown, and he has a
short dark mane and a long dark stripe down his
back as a donkey has, though this last character you
may also see in many of our Devonshire ponies.
Living often on the high plateaux, sometimes as

Fig. 74.

Equus hemionus, " Kiang " or " Kulan," the Horse-ass of
Tartary and Tibet. (Brehm.)

much as 1500 feet above the sea, this "child of the
steppes" travels in large companies even as far as
the rich meadows of Central Asia; in summer
wandering in green pastures, and in winter seeking the
hunger-steppes where sturdy plants grow. And when
autumn comes the young steeds go off alone to the
mountain heights to survey the country around and

call wildly for mates, whom, when found, they will keep close to them through all the next year, even though they mingle with thousands of others.

Till about ten years ago the *Equus hemionus* was the only truly wild horse known, but in the winter of 1879-80 the Russian traveller Przevalsky brought back from Central Asia a much more horse-like animal, called by the Tartars " Kertag " and by the Mongols " Statur."   It is a clumsy, thick-set, whitish-gray creature with strong legs and a large,

Fig. 75.

Przevalsky's Wild Horse, the " Kertag " or " Statur."

heavy, reddish-coloured head ; its legs have a red tint down to the knees, beyond which they are blackish down to the hoofs.   But the ears are small, and it has the broad hoofs of the true horse, and warts on his hind legs, which no animal of the ass tribe has. This horse, like the Kiang, travels in small troops of from five to fifteen, led through the wildest parts of the Dsungarian desert, between the Altai and Tian-schan Mountains, by an old stallion. They are extremely shy, and see, hear, and smell very quickly, so that they are off like lightning whenever anything approaches them.

So having travelled over America, Europe, and Asia, was my quest ended ? No ; for from the dreary Asiatic deserts my thoughts wandered to a far warmer and more fertile land, where between the Blue Nile and the Red Sea rise the lofty highlands of Abyssinia, among which the African wild ass (*Asinus tæniopus*), the probable ancestor of our donkeys, feeds in troops on the rich grasses of the slopes, and then onwards to the bank of a river in Central Africa where on the edge of a forest, with rich pastures beyond, elephants and rhinoceroses, antelopes and buffaloes, lions and hyænas, creep down in the cool of the evening to slake their thirst in the flowing stream. There I saw the herds of Zebras in all their striped beauty coming down from the mountain regions to the north, and ming-ling with the darker-coloured but graceful quaggas from the southern plains, and I half-grieved at the thought how these untamed and free rovers are being slowly but surely surrounded by man closing in upon them on every side.

I might now have travelled still farther in search of the Onager, or wild ass of the Asiatic and Indian deserts, but at this point a more interesting and far wider question presented itself, as I flung myself down on the moor to ponder over the early history of all these tribes.

19

Where have they all come from? Where shall
we ' look for the first ancestors of these wild and
graceful animals? For the answer to this question
I had to travel back to America, to those Western
United States where Professor Marsh has made such
grand discoveries in horse history. For there, in the
very country where horses were supposed never to
have been before the Spaniards brought them a few
centuries ago, we have now found the true birth-
place of the equine race.

Come back with me to a time so remote that we
cannot measure it even by hundreds of thousands of
years, and let us visit the territories of Utah and
Wyoming. Those highlands were very different
then from what they are now. Just risen out of the
seas of the Cretaceous Period, they were then clothed
with dense forests of palms, tree-ferns, and screw-
pines, magnolias and laurels, interspersed with wide-
spreading lakes, on the margins of which strange and
curious animals fed and flourished. There were
large beasts with teeth like the tapir and the bear,
and feet like the elephant; and others far more
dangerous, half bear, half hyæna, prowling around
to attack the clumsy palæotherium or the anoplo-
therium, something between a rhinoceros and a
horse, which grazed by the waterside, while graceful
antelopes fed on the rich grass. And among these
were some little animals no bigger than foxes, with
four toes and a splint for the fifth, on their front
feet, and three toes on the hind ones.

These clumsy little animals, whose bones have
been found in the rocks of Utah and Wyoming,

have been called *Eohippus*, or horses of the dawn, by naturalists. They were animals with real toes, yet their bones and teeth show that they belonged to the horse tribe, and already the fifth toe common to most other toed animals was beginning to disappear.

This was in the Eocene period, and before it passed away with its screw-pines and tree-ferns, another rather larger animal, called the *Orohippus*, had taken the place of the small one, and he had only four toes on his front feet. The splint had disappeared, and as time went on still other animals followed, always with fewer toes, while they gained slender fleet legs, together with an increase in size and in gracefulness. First one as large as a sheep (*Meso-hippus*) had only three toes and a splint. Then the splint again disappeared, and one large and two dwindling toes only remained, till finally these two became mere splints, leaving one large toe or hoof with almost imperceptible splints, which may be seen on the fetlock of a horse's skeleton.

The diagram (Fig 76) shows these splints in the horse's or ass's foot of to-day. For you must notice that a horse's foot really begins at the point *w* which we call his knee in the front legs, and at his hock *h* in the hind legs. His true knee *k* and elbow *e* are close up to the body. What we call his foot or hoof is really the end of the strong, broad, middle toe *t* covered with a hoof, and farther up his foot at *s* and *s* we can feel two small splints, which are remains of two other toes.

Meanwhile during these long succeeding ages while the foot was lengthening out into a slender

limb the animals became larger, more powerful, and
more swift, the neck and head became longer and
more graceful, the brain-case larger in front and the
teeth decreased in number, so that there is now a
large gap between the biting teeth *i* and the grinding

Fig. 76.

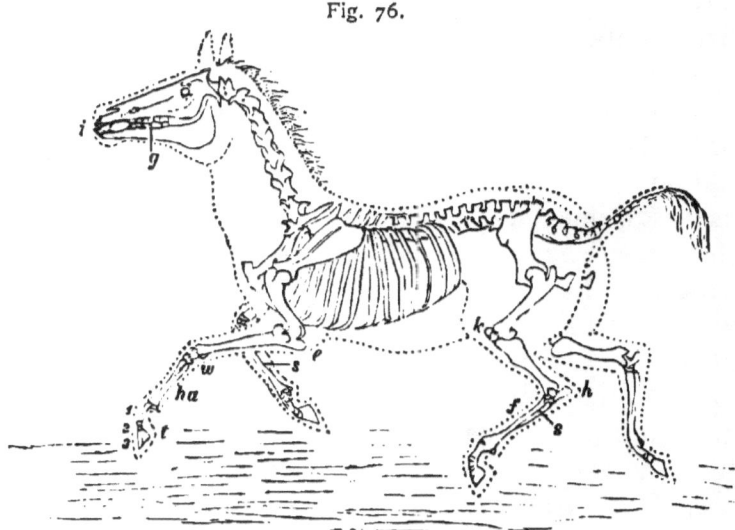

Skeleton of Horse or Ass.

i, Incisor teeth.   *g*, Grinding teeth, with the gap between the two as in
all grass-feeders.   *k*, Knee.   *h*, Hock or heel.   *f*, Foot.   *s*, Splints or
remains of the two lost toes.   *e*, Elbow.   *w*, Wrist.   *h*, Hand-bone.
t, middle toe of three joints, 1, 2, 3 forming the hoof.

teeth *g* of a horse.   Their slender limbs too became
more flexible and fit for running and galloping, till
we find the whole skeleton the same in shape, though
not in size, as in our own horses and asses now.

They did not, however, during all this time remain
confined to America, for, from the time when they
arrived at an animal called *Miohippus*, or lesser

horse, which came after the Mesohippus and had only three toes on each foot, we find their remains in Europe, where they lived in company with the giraffes, opossums, and monkeys which roamed over these parts in those ancient times. Then a little later we find them in Africa and India ; so that the horse tribe, represented by creatures about as large as donkeys, had spread far and wide over the world.

And now, curiously enough, they began to forsake, or to die out in, the land of their birth. Why they did so we do not know ; but while in the old world as asses, quaggas, and zebras, and probably horses, they flourished in Asia, Europe, and Africa, they certainly died out in America, so that ages afterwards, when that land was discovered, no animal of the horse tribe was found in it.

And the true horse, where did he arise ? Born and bred probably in Central Asia from some animal like the " Kulan," or the " Kertag," he proved too useful to savage tribes to be allowed his freedom, and it is doubtful whether in any part of the world he escaped subjection. In our own country he probably roamed as a wild animal till the savages, who fed upon him, learned in time to put him to work ; and when the Romans came they found the Britons with fine and well-trained horses.

Yet though tamed and made to know his master he has, as we have seen, broken loose again in almost all parts of the world—in America on the prairies and pampas, in Europe and Asia on the steppes, and in Australia in the bush. And even in Great Britain, where so few patches of uncultivated land still remain, the young colts of Dartmoor, Exmoor, and Shetland, though born of domesticated mothers, seem to assert their descent from wild and free ancestors as they throw out their heels and toss up their heads with a shrill neigh, and fly against the wind with streaming manes and outstretched tails as the Kulan, the Tarpan, and the Zebra do in the wild desert or grassy plain.

CHAPTER X

HE magician sat in his arm-chair in the one little room in the house which was his, and his only, besides the ob-servatory. And a strange room it was. The walls were hung with skulls and bones of men and animals, with swords, daggers, and shields, coats of mail, and bronze spear - heads. The drawers, many of which stood open, contained flint - stones chipped and worn, arrowheads of stone, jade hatchets beauti-fully polished, bronze buckles and iron armlets; while scattered among these were pieces of broken pottery, some rough and only half-baked, others beautifully finished, as the Romans knew how to finish them. Rough needles made of bone lay beside bronze knives with richly-ornamented handles and, most precious of all, on the table by the magician's side lay a reindeer antler, on which was roughly carved the figure of the reindeer itself.

He had been enjoying a six weeks' holiday, and he had employed it in visiting some of the bone caves of Europe to learn about the men who lived in them long, long ago. He had been to the south of France to see the famous caves of the Dordogne, to Belgium to the caves of Engis and Engihoul, to the Hartz Mountains and to Hungary. Then hastening home he had visited the chief English caves in Yorkshire, Wales, and Devonshire.

Now that he had returned to his college, his mind was so full of facts, that he felt perplexed how to lay before his class the wonderful story of the life of man before history began. And as the day was hot, and the very breeze which played around him made him feel languid and sleepy, he fell into a reverie—a waking dream.

.   .   .   .   .   .

First the room faded from his sight, then the trim villages disappeared ; the homesteads, the corn-fields, the grazing cattle, all were gone, and he saw the whole of England covered with thick forests and rough uncultivated land. From the mountains in the north, glaciers were to be seen creeping down the valleys between dense masses of fir and oak, pine and birch ; while the wild horse, the bison, and the Irish elk were feeding on the plains. As he looked southward and eastward he saw that the sea no longer washed the shores, for the English and Irish Channels were not yet scooped out. The British Isles were still part of the continent of Europe, so that animals could migrate overland from the far south, up to what is now England, Scotland, and Ireland. Many of these animals, too, were very different from any now living in the country, for in the large rivers of England he saw the hippopotamus playing with her calf, while elephants and rhinoceroses were drinking at the water's edge. Yet these strange creatures did not have all the country to themselves—wolves, bears, and foxes prowled in the woods, large beavers built their dams across the streams, and here and there over the country human beings were living in caves and holes of the earth.

It was these men chiefly who attracted the magician's attention, and being curious to know how they lived, he turned towards a cave, at the mouth of which was a group of naked children who were knocking pieces of flint together, trying to strike off splinters and make rough flint tools, such as they saw their fathers use. Not far off from them a woman with a wild beast's skin round her waist was gathering firewood, another was grubbing up roots, and another, venturing a little way into the forest, was searching for honey in the hollows of the tree trunks.

All at once in the dusk of the evening a low growl and a frightened cry were heard, and the women rushed towards the cave as they saw near the edge of the forest a huge tiger with sabre-shaped teeth struggling with a powerful stag. In vain the deer tried to stamp on his savage foe or to wound him with his antlers; the strong teeth of the tiger had penetrated his throat, and they fell struggling

together as the stag uttered his death-cry. Just at
that moment loud shouts were heard in the forest,
and the frightened women knew that help was near.

Fig. 77.

Palæolithic times.

One after another, several men, clothed in skins
hung over one shoulder and secured round the waist,
rushed out of the thicket, their hair streaming in the
wind, and ran towards the tiger.   They held in their
hands strange weapons made of rough pointed flints
fastened into handles by thongs of skin, and as the
tiger turned upon them with a cry of rage they met
him with a rapid shower of blows.   The fight raged

fiercely, for the beast was strong and the weapons of the men were rude, but the tiger lay dead at last by the side of his victim. His skin and teeth were the reward of the hunters, and the stag he had killed became their prey.

How skilfully they hacked it to pieces with their stone axes, and then loading it upon their shoulders set off up the hill towards the cave, where they were welcomed with shouts of joy by the women and children !

Then began the feast. First fires were kindled slowly and with difficulty by rubbing a sharp-pointed stick in a groove of softer wood till the wood-dust burst into flame ; then a huge pile was lighted at the mouth of the cave to cook the food and keep off wild beasts. How the food was cooked the magician could not see, but he guessed that the flesh was cut off the bones and thrust in the glowing embers, and he watched the men afterwards splitting open the

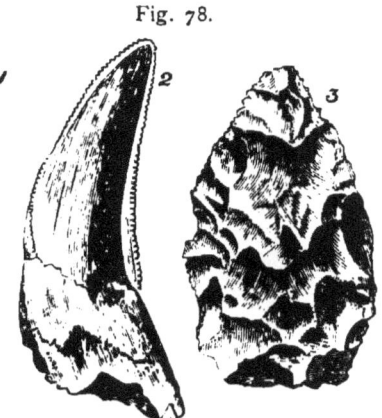

Fig. 78.

Palæolithic relics.

1, Bone needle, from a cave at La Madeleine, ½ size. 2, Tooth of Machairodus or sabre-toothed tiger, from Kent's Cavern, ½ size. 3, Rough stone implement, from Kent's Cavern, ¼ size.

uncooked bones to suck out the raw marrow which savages love.

After the feast was over he noticed how they left

these split bones scattered upon the floor of the cave mingling with the sabre-shaped teeth of the tiger, and this reminded him of the bones of the stag and the tiger's tooth which he had found in Kent's Cavern in Devonshire only a few days before.

By this time the men had lain down to sleep, and in the darkness strange cries were heard from the forest. The roar of the lion, mingled with the howling of the wolves and the shrill laugh of the hyænas, told that they had come down to feed on the remains of the tiger. But none of these animals ventured near the glowing fire at the mouth of the cavern, behind which the men slept in security till the sun was high in the heavens. Then all was astir again, for weapons had been broken in the fight, and some of the men sitting on the ground outside the cave placed one flint between their knees, and striking another sharply against it drove off splinters, leaving a pointed end and cutting edge. They spoiled many before they made one to their liking, and the entrance to the cave was strewn with splintered fragments and spoilt flints, but at last several useful stones were ready. Meanwhile another man, taking his rude stone axe, set to work to hew branches from the trees to form handles, while another, choosing a piece remaining of the body of the stag, tore a sinew from the thigh, and threading it through the large eye of the bone needle, stitched the tiger's skin roughly together into a garment.

" *This, then,*" said the magician to himself, " *is how ancient man lived in the summer-time, but how would he fare when winter came ?* " As he mused the scene gradually changed. The glaciers crept far lower down the valleys, and the hills, and even the lower ground, lay thick in snow. The hippopotamus had wandered away southward to warmer climes, as animals now migrate over the continent of America in winter, and with him had gone the lion, the southern elephant, and other summer visitors. In their place large herds of reindeer and shaggy oxen had come down from the north and were spread over the plains, scraping away the snow with their feet to feed on the grass beneath. The mammoth, too, or hairy elephant, of the same extinct species as those which have been found frozen in solid ice under a sandbank in Siberia, had come down to feed, accompanied by the woolly rhinoceros ; and scattered over the hills were the curious horned musk-sheep, which have long ago disappeared off the face of the earth. Still, bitterly cold as it was, the hunter clad in his wild-beast skin came out from time to time to chase the mammoth, the reindeer, and the oxen for food, and cut wood in the forest to feed the cavern fires.

This time the magician's thoughts wandered down to the south-west of France, where, on the banks of a river in that part now called the Dordogne, a number of caves not far from each other formed the home of savage man. Here he saw many new things, for the men used arrows of deer-horn and of wood pointed with flint, and with these they shot the birds, which were hovering near in hopes of finding food during the bitter weather. By the side of the river a man was throwing a small dart of

20

deer-horn fastened to a cord of sinews, with which
from time to time he speared a large fish and drew
it to the bank.

But the most curious sight of all, among such a
rude people, was a man sitting by the glowing fire at
the mouth of one of the caves scratching a piece of
reindeer horn with a pointed flint, while the children
gathered round him to watch his work. What was
he doing? See! gradually the rude scratches began
to take shape, and two reindeer fighting together
could be recognised upon the horn handle. This
he laid carefully aside, and taking a piece of ivory,
part of the tusk of a mammoth, he worked away

Fig. 79.

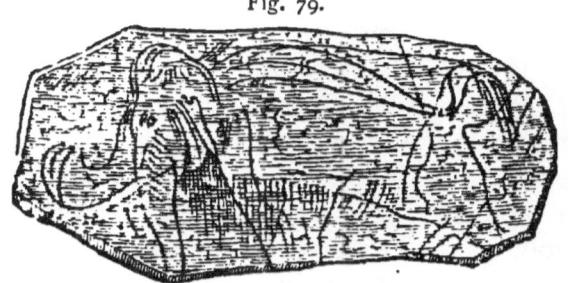

Mammoth engraved on ivory by Palæolithic man.

slowly and carefully till the children grew tired of
watching and went off to play behind the fire. Then
the magician, glancing over his shoulder, saw a true
figure of the mammoth scratched upon the ivory,
his hairy skin, long mane, and up-curved tusks dis-
tinguishing him from all elephants living now. "*Ah*,"
exclaimed the magician aloud, "*that is the drawing
on ivory found in the cave of La Madeleine in Dordogne, proving that man existed ages ago, and even*

knew how to draw figures, at a time when the mam-
moth, or hairy elephant, long since extinct, was still
living on the earth !"

With these words he started from his reverie, and
knew that he had been dreaming of Palæolithic man
who, with his tools of rough flints, had lived in
Europe so long ago that his date cannot be fixed by
years, or centuries, or even thousands of years.
Only this is known, that, since he lived, the mammoth, the sabre-toothed tiger, the cave-bear, the
woolly rhinoceros, the cave-hyæna, the musk-sheep,
and many other animals have died out from off the
face of the earth ; the hippopotamus and the lion
have left Europe and retired to Africa, and the sea has
flowed in where land once was, cutting off Great
Britain and Ireland from the continent.

How long all these changes were in taking place
no one knows. When the magician drifted back
again into his dream the land had long been
desolate, and the hyænas, which had always taken
possession of the caves whenever the men deserted
them for awhile, had now been undisturbed for a
long time, and had left on the floor of the cave
gnawed skulls and bones, and jaws of animals, more
or less scored with the marks of their teeth, and
these had become buried in a thick layer of earth.
The magician knew that these teeth marks had been
made by hyænas, both because living hyænas leave
exactly such marks on bones in the present day, and
because the hyæna bones alone were not gnawed,
showing that no animals preyed upon their flesh. He
knew too that the hyænas had been there long after

man had ceased to use the caves, because no flint
tools were found among the bones. But now the
age of hyænas, too, was past and gone, and the caves
had been left so long undisturbed that in many of
them the water dripping from the roof had left film
after film of carbonate of lime upon the floor, which
as the centuries went by became a layer of stalag-
mite many feet thick, sealing down the secrets of the
past.   .   .   .   .

The face of the country was now entirely changed.
The glaciers were gone, and so, too, were all the
strange animals. True, the reindeer, the wild ox,
and even here and there the Irish elk, were still feeding in the valleys ; wolves and bears still made the
country dangerous, and beavers built their dams
across the streams, which were now much smaller
than formerly, and flowed in deeper channels, carved
out by water during the interval ; but the elephants,
rhinoceroses, lions, and tigers were gone never to
return, and near the caves in which some of the
people lived, and the rude underground huts which
formed the homes of others, tame sheep and goats
were lying with dogs to watch them. Also, though
the land was still covered with dense forests, yet here
and there small clearings had been made, where
patches of corn and flax were growing. Naked
children still played about as before, but now they
were moulding cups of clay like those in which food
was being cooked on the fire outside the caves or
huts. Some of the women, dressed partly in skins
of beasts, partly in rough woven linen, were spinning

flax into thread, using as a spinning-whorl a small round stone with a hole in the middle tied to the end of the flax, as a weight to enable them to twirl it. Others were grinding corn in the hollow of a large stone by rubbing another stone within it.

The men, while they still spent much time in hunting, had now other duties in tending the sheep and goats, or looking after the hogs as they turned up the ground in the forest for roots, or sowing and reaping their crops. Yet still all the tools were made of stone, no longer rough and merely chipped like the old stone weapons, but neatly cut and

Fig. 80.

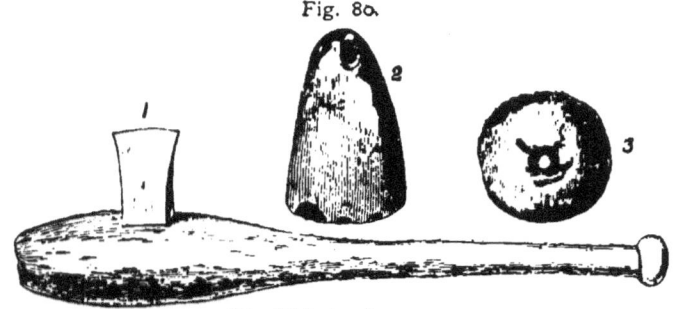

Neolithic implements.

1, Stone hatchet mounted in wood. 2, Jade celt, a polished stone weapon, from Livermore in Suffolk, ¼ size. 3, Spindle whorl, ½ size.

polished. Stone axes with handles of deer-horn, stone spears and javelins, stone arrowheads beautifully finished, sling-stones and scrapers, were among their weapons and tools, and with them they made many delicate implements of bone. On the broad lakes which here and there broke the monotony of the forests, canoes, made of the trunks of trees hollowed out by fire, were being paddled by one man, while another threw out his fishing line armed with delicate bone-hooks ; and on the banks of the lakes, nets weighted with drilled stones tied on to the meshes were dragged up full of fish.

For these Neolithic men, or men of the New Stone Period, who used polished stone weapons, were farmers and shepherds and fishermen. They knew how to make rude pottery, and kept domestic animals. Moreover, they either came from the east or exchanged goods by barter with tribes living more to the eastward, now that canoes enabled them to cross the sea ; for many of their weapons were made of greenstone or jade, and of other kinds of stone not to be found in Europe, and their sheep and goats were animals of eastern origin. They understood how to unite to protect their homes, for they made underground huts by digging down several feet into the ground and roofing the hole over with wood coated with clay ; and often long passages underground united these huts, while in many places on the hills, camps, made of ramparts of earth surrounded by ditches, served as strongholds for the women and children and the flocks and herds, when some neighbouring tribe attacked their homesteads.

Still, however, where caves were ready to hand they used them for houses, and the same shelter which had been the home of the ancient hunters, now resounded with the voices of the shepherds, who, treading on the sealed floor, little dreamt that under their feet lay the remains of a bygone age.

And now, as our dreamer watched this new race

of men fashioning their weapons, feeding their oxen, and hunting the wild stag, his attention was arrested by a long train of people crossing a neighbouring plain, weeping and wailing as they went. At the head of this procession, lying on a stretcher made of

Fig. 81.

A burial in Neolithic times.

tree-boughs, lay a dead chieftain, and as the line moved on, men threw down their tools, and women their spinning, and joined the throng. On they went to where two upright slabs of stone with another laid across them formed the opening to a long mound or chamber. Into this the bearers passed with lighted torches, and in a niche ready prepared placed the dead chieftain in a sitting posture with the knees drawn up, placing by his side his flint spear and polished axe, his necklace of shells, and the bowl from which he had fed. Then followed the funeral feast, when, with shouts and wailing, fires were lighted, and animals slaughtered and cooked, while the chieftain was not forgotten, but portions were left for his use, and then the earth was piled up again around the mouth of the chamber, till it should be opened at some future time to place another member of his family by his side, or till in after ages the antiquary should rifle his resting-place to study the mode of burial in the Neolithic or Polished Stone Age.

. Time passed on in the magician's dream, and little by little the caves were entirely deserted as men learnt to build huts of wood and stone. And as they advanced in knowledge they began to melt metals and pour them into moulds, making bronze knives and hatchets, swords and spears; and they fashioned brooches and bracelets of bronze and gold, though they still also used their necklaces of shells and their polished stone weapons. They began, too, to keep ducks and fowls, cows and horses; they knew how to weave in looms, and to make cloaks and tunics; and when they buried their dead it was no longer in a crouching position. They laid them decently to rest, as if in sleep, in the barrows where they are found to this day with bronze weapons by their side.

Then as time went on they learnt to melt even hard iron, and to beat it into swords and ploughshares, and they lived in well-built huts with stone foundations. Their custom of burial, too, was again changed, and they burnt their dead, placing the ashes in a funeral urn.

By this time the Britons, as they were now called, had begun to gather together in villages and towns, and the Romans ruled over them. Now when men passed through the wild country they were often finely

Fig. 82.

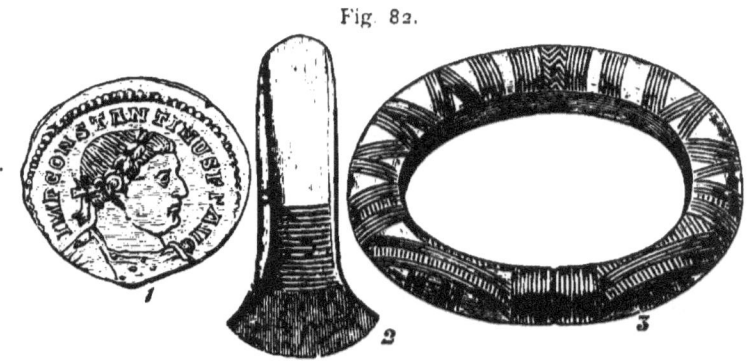

British relics.

1, A coin of the age of Constantine. 2, Bronze weapon from a Suffolk barrow. 3, Bronze bracelet from Liss in Hampshire.

dressed in cloth tunics, wearing arm rings of gold, some even driving in war-chariots, carrying shields made of wickerwork covered with leather. Still many of the country people who laboured in the field kept their old clothing of beast skins; they grew their corn and stored it in cavities of the rocks; they made basket-work boats covered with skin, in which they ventured out to sea. So things went on for a long period till at last a troubled time came, and the quiet valleys were disturbed by wandering people who fled

from the towns and took refuge in the forests ; for
the Romans after three hundred and fifty years of
rule had gone back home to Italy, and a new and
barbarous people called the Jutes, Angles, and
Saxons, came over the sea from Jutland and drove
the Britons from their homes.

And so once more the caves became the abode of
man, for the harassed Britons brought what few things

Fig. 83.

Britons taking refuge in the Cave.

they could carry away from their houses and hid
themselves there from their enemies. How little
they thought, as they lay down to sleep on the
cavern floor, that beneath them lay the remains of

two ages of men! They knew nothing of the
woman who had dropped her stone spindle-whorl
into the fire, on which the food of Neolithic man
had been cooking in rough pots of clay ; they never
dug down to the layer of gnawed bones, nor did
they even in their dreams picture the hyæna haunt-
ing his ancient den, for a hyæna was an animal
they had never seen. Still less would they have
believed that at one time, countless ages before,
their island had been part of the continent, and
that men, living in the cave where they now lay,
had cut down trees with rough flints, and fought
with such unknown animals as the mammoth and
the sabre-toothed tiger.

But the magician saw it all passing before him,
even as he also saw these Britons carrying into the
cave their brooches, bracelets, and finger rings, their
iron spears and bronze daggers, and all their little
household treasures which they had saved in their
flight. And among these, mingling in the heap, he
recognised Roman coins bearing the inscription of
the Emperor Constantine, and he knew that it was
by these coins that he had, a few days before in
Yorkshire, been able to fix the date of the British
occupation of a cave.

.   .   .

And with this his dream ended, and he found
himself clutching firmly the horn on which Palæolithic man had engraved the figure of the reindeer.
He rose, and stretching himself crossed the sunny
grass plot of the quadrangle and entered his class-
room. The boys wondered as he began his lecture

at the far-away look in his eyes.   They did not know how he had passed through a vision of countless ages ; but that afternoon, for the first time, they realised, as he unfolded scene after scene, the history of " The Men of Ancient Days."

INDEX

21

THE END

*A*ROUND AND ABOUT SOUTH AMERICA : *Twenty Months of Quest and Query.* By FRANK VINCENT, author of "The Land of the White Elephant," etc. With Maps, Plans, and 54 full-page Illustrations. 8vo, xxiv–473 pages. Ornamental cloth, $5.00.

No former traveler has made so comprehensive and thorough a tour of Spanish and Portuguese America as did Mr. Vincent. He visited every capital, chief city, and important seaport, made several expeditions into the interior of Brazil and the Argentine Republic, and ascended the Paraná, Paraguay, Amazon, Orinoco, and Magdalena Rivers; he visited the crater of Pichincha, 16,000 feet above the sea-level; he explored falls in the center of the continent, which, though meriting the title of "Niagara of South America," are all but unknown to the outside world; he spent months in the picturesque capital of Rio Janeiro; he visited the coffee districts, studied the slaves, descended the gold-mines, viewed the greatest rapids of the globe, entered the isolated Guianas, and so on.

*B*RAZIL: *Its Condition and Prospects.* By C. C. ANDREWS, ex-Consul-General to Brazil. 12mo. Cloth, $1.50.

"I hope I may be able to present some facts in respect to the present situation of Brazil which will be both instructive and entertaining to general readers. My means of acquaintance with that empire are principally derived from a residence of three years at Rio de Janeiro, its capital, while employed in the service of the United States Government, during which period I made a few journeys into the interior."—*From the Preface.*

*F*IVE THOUSAND MILES IN A SLEDGE: A *Mid-Winter Journey across Siberia.* By LIONEL F. GOWING. With Map and 30 Illustrations in Text. 12mo. Cloth, $1.50.

"The book is most certainly one to be read, and will be welcomed as an addition to the scant literature on a singularly interesting country."—*Courier.*

*C*HINA : *Travels and Investigations in the "Middle Kingdom."* A Study of its Civilization and Possibilities. With a Glance at Japan. By JAMES HARRISON WILSON, late Major-General United States Volunteers and Brevet Major-General United States Army. 12mo. Cloth, $1.75.

"The book presents China and Japan in all these aspects; the manners and customs of the people; the institutions, tendencies, and social ideas; the government and leading men."—*Boston Traveller.*

New York : D. APPLETON & CO., 1, 3, & 5 Bond Street.

THE GARDEN'S STORY; or, Pleasures and Trials of an Amateur Gardener. By GEORGE H. ELLWANGER. With Head and Tail Pieces by Rhead. 12mo. Cloth extra, $1.50.

"Mr. Ellwanger's instinct rarely errs in matters of taste. He writes out of the fullness of experimental knowledge, but his knowledge differs from that of many a trained cultivator in that his skill in garden practice is guided by a refined æsthetic sensibility, and his appreciation of what is beautiful in nature is healthy, hearty, and catholic. His record of the garden year, as we have said, begins with the earliest violet, and it follows the season through until the witch-hazel is blossoming on the border of the wintry woods. . . . This little book can not fail to give pleasure to all who take a genuine interest in rural life. They will sympathize with most of the author's robust and positive judgments. and with his strong aversions as well as his tender attachments."—*The Tribune*, New York.

THE FOLK-LORE OF PLANTS. By T. F. THISELTON DYER, M. A. 12mo. Cloth, $1.50.

"The Folk-Lore of Plants" traces the superstitions and fancies connected with plants in fairy-lore, in witchcraft and demonology, in religion. in charms. in medicine, in plant language. etc. The author is an eminent English botanist. and superintendent of the gardens at Kew.

"A handsome and deeply interesting volume. . . . In all respects the book is excellent. Its arrangement is simple and intelligible, its style bright and alluring. authorities are cited at the foot of the page. and a full index is appended. . . . To all who seek an introduction to one of the most attractive branches of folk-lore, this delightful volume may be warmly commended."—*Notes and Queries*.

FLOWERS AND THEIR PEDIGREES. By GRANT ALLEN, author of "Vignettes of Nature." etc. Illustrated. 12mo. Cloth, $1.50.

No writer treats scientific subjects with so much ease and charm of style as Mr. Grant Allen. His sketches in the magazines have well been called fascinating, and the present volume, being a collection of various papers, will fully sustain his reputation as an eminently entertaining and suggestive writer.

"'Flowers and their Pedigrees,' by Grant Allen. with many illustrations, is not merely a description of British wild flowers. but a discussion of why they are, what they are, and how they come to be so, in other words. a scientific study of the migration and transformation of plants. illustrated by the daisy. the strawberry. the cleavers, wheat, the mountain tulip, the cuckoo-pint, and a few others. The study is a delightful one, and the book is fascinating to any one who has either love for flowers or curiosity about them."—*Hartford Courant*.

New York: D. APPLETON & CO., 1, 3, & 5 Bond Street.

THE HISTORY OF ANCIENT CIVILIZATION.

A Hand-book based upon M. Gustave Ducoudray's "Histoire Sommaire de la Civilisation." Edited by the Rev. J. VERSCHOYLE, M. A. With numerous Illustrations. Large 12mo. Cloth, $1.75.

"With M. Ducoudray's work as a basis, many additions having been made, derived from special writers, Mr. Verschoyle has produced an excellent work, which gives a comprehensive view of early civilization. . . . As to the world of the past, the volume under notice treats of Egypt, Assyria, the Far East, of Greece and Rome in the most comprehensive manner. It is not the arts alone which are fully illustrated, but the literature, laws, manners, and customs, the beliefs of all these countries are contrasted. If the book gave alone the history of the monuments of the past it would be valuable, but it is its all-around character which renders it so useful. A great many volumes have been produced treating of a past civilization, but we have seen none which in the same space gives such varied information."—*The New York Times.*

GREAT LEADERS: Historic Portraits from the Great Historians.

Selected, with Notes and Brief Biographical Sketches, by G. T. FERRIS. With sixteen engraved Portraits. 12mo. Cloth, $1.75.

The Historic Portraits of this work are eighty in number, drawn from the writings of PLUTARCH, GROTE, GIBBON, CURTIUS, MOMMSEN, FROUDE, HUME, MACAULAY, LECKY, GREEN, THIERS, TAINE, PRESCOTT, MOTLEY, and other historians. The subjects extend from Themistocles to Wellington.

"Every one perusing the pages of the historians must have been impressed with the graphic and singularly penetrative character of many of the sketches of the distinguished persons whose doings form the staple of history. These pen-portraits often stand out from the narrative with luminous and vivid effect, the writers seeming to have concentrated upon them all their powers of penetration and all their skill in graphic delineation. Few things in literature are marked by analysis so close, discernment so keen, or effects so brilliant and dramatic."—*From the Preface.*

LIFE OF THE GREEKS AND ROMANS, described from Ancient Monuments.

By E. GUHL and W. KONER. Translated from the third German edition by F. HUEFFER. With 543 Illustrations. 8vo. Cloth, $2.50.

"The result of careful and unwearied research in every nook and cranny of ancient learning. Nowhere else can the student find so many facts in illustration of Greek and Roman methods and manners."—*Dr. C. K. Adams's Manual of Historical Literature.*

New York: D. APPLETON & CO., 1, 3, & 5 Bond Street.

www.ingramcontent.com/pod-product-compliance
Lightning Source LLC
Chambersburg PA
CBHW030801020726
47499CB00006B/1723